"I can't g

"Why not?"

"For starters, you work for me."

"Okay, I quit."

Jewel laughed, though the intensity with which he was staring at her made her suspect that he wasn't entirely joking.

"Anyway, you lost the race."

"You cheated."

She lifted a brow. "How do you figure?"

"You started first."

"Just because you were slow out of the gate—"

The rest of the words lodged in her throat when his arm snaked around her waist. "No one's ever accused me of being slow out of the gate."

"Well—" she gave herself a moment to acknowledge the delicious little sparks that zinged through her system "—you were this time."

"Maybe I was," he acknowledged, drawing her closer. "Or maybe I chose finesse over speed."

"You still lost."

He smiled. "I don't think so."

Then he kissed her.

Dear Reader,

Do opposites really attract?

That was the question I asked myself when I sat down to write *The Prince's Cowgirl Bride*. After all, what could a Harvard-educated lawyer masquerading as a stable hand have in common with a former rodeo champion turned horse trainer? Is it really possible that two such disparate characters could fall in love and find a happily-ever-after together?

Factor in that the hero is several years younger than the object of his affections, lives in a different country and forgot to mention to his new boss that he's royalty, and, well, obviously this couple has some issues to work through.

But maybe love can conquer all. And maybe wedding bells will be ringing again soon in Tesoro del Mar....

I hope you enjoy Marcus and Jewel's story!

Best,

Brenda Harlen

THE PRINCE'S COWGIRL BRIDE

BRENDA HARLEN

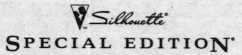

SPECIAL EDITION

Published by Silhouette Books

America's Publisher of Contemporary Romance

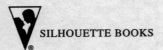

SILHOUETTE BOOKS

ISBN-13: 978-0-373-24920-6
ISBN-10:   0-373-24920-9

THE PRINCE'S COWGIRL BRIDE

Books by Brenda Harlen

Silhouette Special Edition

Once and Again #1714
*Her Best-Kept Secret #1756
The Marriage Solution #1811
†*One Man's Family* #1827
The New Girl in Town #1859
**The Prince's Royal Dilemma #1898
**The Prince's Cowgirl Bride #1920

Silhouette Romantic Suspense

McIver's Mission #1224
Some Kind of Hero #1246
Extreme Measures #1282
Bulletproof Hearts #1313
Dangerous Passions #1394

*Family Business
†Logan's Legacy Revisited
**Reigning Men

BRENDA HARLEN

grew up in a small town surrounded by books and imaginary friends. Although she always dreamed of being a writer, she chose to follow a more traditional career path first. After two years of practicing as an attorney (including an appearance in front of the Supreme Court of Canada), she gave up her "real" job to be a mom and to try her hand at writing books. Three years, five manuscripts and another baby later, she sold her first book—an RWA Golden Heart winner—to Silhouette Books.

Brenda lives in Southern Ontario with her real-life husband/hero, two heroes-in-training and two neurotic dogs. She is still surrounded by books ("too many books," according to her children) and imaginary friends, but she also enjoys communicating with "real" people. Readers can contact Brenda by e-mail at brendaharlen@yahoo.com or by snail mail c/o Silhouette Books, 233 Broadway, Suite 1001, New York, NY 10279.

For Connor & Ryan
—the next generation of princes—
the reason for everything I do.

I love you both
with all of my heart.

Prologue

"Does it give you ideas?"

Prince Marcus Santiago of Tesoro del Mar glanced down at his dance partner and found her smiling up at him with big blue eyes filled with promises she was far too young to be making. He'd been holding her at a careful distance, not wanting to give her any encouragement or the press any reason to speculate that he was interested in more than waltzing with a guest at his brother's wedding, but clearly she hadn't taken the hint.

"No." His answer was succinct and unequivocal.

"I'll bet if you met the right woman you'd change your mind."

"Maybe if I met her at the right time," he conceded, though he sincerely doubted it. "But I've got to finish university before I even start thinking about settling down."

She pouted prettily. "Are you really going back to Harvard next week?"

"Only because the university has this annoying expectation that a student attend classes and write exams in order to earn a degree."

She laughed prettily. "But you're not *really* going to be a lawyer."

"Aren't I?"

"Of course not. You're a prince."

"The two titles aren't mutually exclusive," he said dryly.

Her eyelashes fluttered. "I only meant that you don't need to work."

He couldn't prevent the smile that curved his lips. Clearly this girl had no idea what it meant to be a royal. The truth was, he didn't know anyone who worked harder or longer than his brother Rowan. As the youngest, Marcus didn't bear the same burden of responsibilities, but he wasn't exactly given a free ride, either.

She shifted closer to him, lowered her voice. "If you must go away, maybe we could go somewhere to share a private goodbye."

He was relieved to note that the song was winding down to a finish. He touched his lips briefly to the back of her hand and stepped back. "Right now, I must speak with my brother."

Disappointment clouded her eyes as she dropped into a curtsy. "Of course, Your Highness. Maybe later?"

He didn't bother to respond.

That was exactly why Marcus wasn't a big fan of weddings. It wasn't so much that he was opposed to the institution of marriage—not for other people, anyway. No, what he disliked was the effect that they seemed to have on the single females in attendance. It was as if they suddenly couldn't see anything but wedding gowns and bouquets of flowers and any unmarried man who happened in their path as a potential candidate for the altar. No thank you—no way.

There were just too many women out there—fun women, smart women, beautiful women—to want to commit to a single one. If he ever met a woman who was all of those things, he might reconsider his attitude toward matrimony, but he was doubtful.

He snagged a glass of champagne from the tray of a passing waiter and carried it to the terrace where he'd seen his brother Eric disappear. He found him in the shadows, nursing a drink of his own.

"Hiding out?" Marcus asked him.

Eric grinned. "And not ashamed to admit it."

He leaned back against the stone balustrade and crossed his feet at the ankles. "So how many times have you been asked if Rowan's wedding has given you ideas about getting married?"

"I lost count."

Marcus nodded and sipped his champagne, enjoying the stolen moment of quiet camaraderie with his brother.

Then Eric broke the silence by saying, "I wouldn't say I've never thought of it, though."

Marcus nearly choked. "Marriage?"

His brother nodded. "Not with respect to any particular woman, but I've wondered, sometimes, what it would be like to have what Julian had with Catherine, or what Rowan has found with Lara."

"*Mi Dios*—don't let anyone overhear you saying that or you'll have a ring on your finger before you have a chance to recover from this temporary bout of insanity."

Eric's lips curved. "Do you really think it's crazy? Crazier than being alone?"

"Maybe you have been at sea too long."

"And that is exactly why I won't ever have what our brother has. Because I can't imagine ever leaving the navy any more than I could imagine asking someone to share my life when I'm at sea more than I'm home."

"You could ask," Marcus argued. "And not have any trouble finding someone who believes becoming a princess is more than adequate compensation for an absent husband."

Eric shook his head. "You're too cynical."

"Realistic. Isn't that why we all have passports with our mother's maiden name—so we can occasionally escape the attention of being royal?"

"I didn't think you minded the attention."

He couldn't blame his brother for thinking that because there had been a time when it was true, when he'd not only not minded the attention but had courted it. Lately, however, he'd just wanted to get away from it all. To shake free of the media spotlight and everyone else's expectations and figure out what he really wanted. Because the truth was, he still didn't have a clue. For too long, he'd been moving from one thing to the next, from school to school, earning degree upon degree, searching for the one thing that really seemed to fit.

Or maybe Eric was right. Maybe it wasn't some*thing* so much as some*one* that he'd been searching for.

He almost laughed out loud at the ridiculousness of that thought.

Tonight, the only thing he was searching for was a good time. He tossed back the rest of his champagne and went to find it.

Chapter One

Two years later...

Jewel Callahan slid onto a stool at the counter at the Halfway Café and scowled at the slim back of the blond woman who was grinding beans for a fresh pot of coffee. Crystal Vasicek was the proprietor of the popular little café and the creator of the most amazingly decadent desserts in all of West Virginia— and probably the other forty-nine states, too.

Jewel waited for the grinder to shut off before she spoke. "It's your fault, you know."

Crystal dumped the grounds into the waiting basket and slid it into place, then punched the button to start the coffee brewing before she turned. "That's quite an accusation coming from the woman who's always so quick to assume responsibility for everyone else's troubles." Her pretty blue eyes sparkled with a combination of amusement and curiosity. "What did I do?"

"It's what you didn't do," Jewel told her.

"Okay—" Crystal picked up a pot of coffee that had finished brewing and poured her sister a cup "—what *didn't* I do?"

"Marry Russ."

Crystal raised a perfectly arched eyebrow. "He never asked."

"He might have." Jewel dumped a heaping spoonful of sugar into her cup. "If you hadn't run off and married Simon."

"Forgive me for falling in love and not anticipating how that event might somehow interfere with your plans."

"You always were the type to leap without looking."

"And you always exercised enough caution for both of us," Crystal replied evenly.

Because she'd wanted to protect her sister, to shield her from the expectations—and the disappointments—that were inherent in being a daughter of Jack Callahan. After all, she'd had half a dozen years of experience with that before Crystal came along.

"We were talking about Russ," Jewel reminded her.

"What about Russ?"

"He's leaving."

"Oh."

There was a wealth of understanding in that single syllable.

Jewel's throat was suddenly tight, making it difficult for her to speak. And what more could she say, anyway?

Crystal went to the bakery display and pulled out a mile-high chocolate cake, then cut a thick wedge and put it on a plate with a fork. Jewel managed a smile as her sister nudged it across the counter toward her. Crystal believed that chocolate was a cure-all for every one of life's problems, and judging by the seven layers of moist cake and creamy icing she'd just set in front of Jewel, she understood the magnitude of this one.

Russ Granger had worked at the Callahan Thoroughbred Center for the last ten years, but he'd been Jewel's friend a lot longer than that, and she couldn't help but be shocked by his defection. He wasn't just leaving his job—he was leaving her. He was the only man she'd ever felt she could truly count on, and now he was moving on.

After pouring herself a cup of coffee, Crystal came around to sit next to her sister at the counter. "Why is he leaving?"

Jewel picked up the fork and dipped the tines into the decadent dark icing. "Because Riley got some big recording contract and he wants to go on tour with her."

"She was wasting her talent singing at The Mustang," Crystal said gently.

Jewel popped a bite of cake into her mouth, but even the rich flavor didn't lift her spirits. "I should have guessed something like this would happen," she admitted. "As soon as he told me he was going to propose to Riley, I should have known. But I was so happy for him that I didn't think about what it might mean for CTC. I certainly didn't think he'd take off in the middle of the season."

"He's leaving soon, then?"

"The end of next week. He's been working closely with Darrell over the past several years and assured me that he's more than ready to take over his duties, but—" she sighed and dug into the cake again "—I can't imagine how I'll get through the season without him."

"You will," Crystal said confidently. "Because there isn't anything you can't do if you put your mind to it."

Jewel had always prided herself on being capable and independent, able to handle anything and everything on her own. And it was a good thing, too, because that was how she always ended up—on her own.

"Jack Callahan might have built CTC, but the only reason it's one of the top training facilities in the state today is because of you," Crystal said, then smiled wryly. "And in spite of me. Lord knows, I never had any interest in staying on the farm or working with the horses."

"You carved your own path." Jewel was proud of her sister's success, and she still got a kick out of the fact that Crystal's spectacular desserts were available not just at the little café where she'd first started baking but in some of the area's trendiest and most exclusive restaurants. "Sometimes I wonder why I couldn't have wanted something else more than I wanted the farm."

"You were a champion barrel racer for three years running," Crystal reminded her.

She smiled, though her memories of that time in her life were more bitter than sweet. "That was a lifetime ago."

"It was what inspired me to do my own thing, regardless of what Jack wanted."

"I would have done anything he wanted," Jewel admitted. Even now, she wasn't sure why she'd always tried so hard to please him, she only knew that she'd never succeeded. Nothing she'd ever done was good enough for Jack Callahan.

"And did," her sister reminded her. "Including giving up your own life to come home when he asked you to."

He hadn't really asked but demanded, as both sisters knew was his way. But the truth was, six years on the rodeo circuit had disillusioned Jewel about a lot of things, and she'd been more than ready to return to Alliston, West Virginia. Her father's heart attack had been both her incentive and her excuse to finally do so and, her difficulties with him aside, she hadn't ever regretted that decision.

She had become his willing assistant, as eager to learn as she was to demonstrate what she already knew, confident that he would learn to trust in her abilities and eventually grant her more authority. But Jack Callahan had continued to hold the reins of the business in his tightly clenched fist until—many years later—they'd finally been pried from his cold, dead fingers.

Jewel and Crystal had stood side by side at his funeral, his daughters from two separate marriages, both sisters painfully aware that they'd been neither wanted nor loved by their father. And more than they'd mourned his death, they'd mourned the distance between them that he'd never tried to breach.

"My life was always here," Jewel finally responded to her sister's comment. "Even when I thought it wasn't."

Crystal touched a hand to her arm. "Maybe the problem isn't that Russ is leaving, but that he found someone and you haven't."

Jewel pushed the half-eaten cake away. "Not this again."

"Honey, you're too young to have resigned yourself to being alone."

"Resigned suggests that I'm settling for less than I want, and I'm not. I'm happy with my life."

"You're happy being alone?"

"I'm hardly alone."

"The horses don't count," her sister said dryly.

"At least they don't hog the bed—or the remote."

"Well, I can't dispute that Simon does both of those things," Crystal said, then a slow smile curved her lips. "But he does other things that more than even the scales—and I'm not talking about taking out the garbage."

Jewel got up and went around the counter to grab the coffeepot for a refill. "You lucked out with Simon," she admitted.

"Then you're not really mad that I didn't wait around for Russ to propose?"

She sighed. "How can I be mad when you're so happy?"

"I am happy," Crystal said. "Happier than I ever could have imagined."

Jewel knew the feeling. She'd experienced that same euphoria of love—and the complete devastation of losing the man she'd thought she would love forever. She only hoped her sister would never have to know that kind of pain, that her life would always be wonderful, that Simon would always love her as much as he did now.

As if following the path of her thoughts, Crystal reached out and squeezed her hand. "Someday your prince will come."

Before Jewel could respond, the jingle of the bell over the door announced the arrival of another customer.

Crystal glanced over, then let out a low whistle.

"Don't look now," she told her sister. "But I think he just walked in the door."

Jewel picked up her cup, sipped.

Crystal frowned at the lack of response.

"You told me not to look," Jewel reminded her.

"Since when do you listen to me?"

She shrugged. "Since the last prince turned into a frog."

Crystal picked up a menu and fanned herself with it. "Six-two, I'd guess. Dark hair, darker eyes. Sinfully sexy.

And—" she glanced pointedly at her sister and smiled "—flying solo."

Her curiosity undeniably piqued by the description, Jewel twisted in her stool—and nearly slid right off of it and onto the floor.

For once, Crystal hadn't exaggerated. The man hovering just inside the door had short, neatly cropped hair, dark slashing brows over espresso-covered eyes, a strong jaw, straight nose, slashing cheekbones and a beautifully sculpted mouth that brought to mind all kinds of wicked fantasies. His olive-toned skin and exotic looks suggested some kind of Mediterranean heritage that made her think of sultry nights and hotter passions, and the punch of lust that hit low in her belly left Jewel almost breathless.

No, her sister definitely hadn't exaggerated. But what she'd neglected to include in her description was "young." Way too young. Probably younger than Crystal even. Definitely too young to make a thirty-four-year-old woman weak in the knees and hot everywhere else.

His gaze moved around the room and collided with hers. Then those beautiful lips slowly curved, and her heart pounded hard against her chest as if it was trying to break free in order to fall at his feet.

"Well, well, well," Crystal said softly.

Jewel felt heat infuse her cheeks as she tore her gaze away from his hypnotic stare. Crystal smirked at her before turning her attention back to the new customer.

"Grab a seat anywhere you like," she called out cheerily. "I'll be with you in just a sec."

"Thank you." His voice was low and deep and as sexy as the rest of him.

"Mmm-mmm," Crystal murmured her appreciation.

Jewel picked up her cup again and sipped before asking, "Weren't we just talking about how happily married you are?"

"I am," Crystal assured her. "But the ring on my finger hasn't affected my eyesight and that is one exceptional specimen of masculinity."

She could hardly deny the fact, nor would she make the mistake of agreeing with her sister aloud, so she only said, "A specimen probably waiting for a cup of coffee."

"Oh. Right." Crystal grinned and grabbed the pot.

Jewel concentrated on finishing her own cup while her sister chatted with her new customer. She couldn't hear what was said, but the low timbre of his voice was enough to create shivers that danced up and down her spine. Crystal's responding laughter bubbled over like a newly opened bottle of champagne, then his deeper chuckle joined in.

Jewel had always envied her sister's ease with other people—her outgoing personality and easy charm, her natural warmth and friendliness. She'd always been more cautious and reserved than Crystal, and though she didn't think anyone would accuse her of being unfriendly, she wasn't often mistaken for warm and welcoming, either. She dealt with a lot of people in her business, not out of choice but necessity, and most of the time, she preferred the horses to their owners. Though lately, she'd been spending a little too much time up close and personal with certain aspects of the thoroughbred training business that she'd prefer to avoid, which reminded her of the other reason she'd come into town to see her sister today.

She waited while Crystal finished serving her "exceptional specimen" and checked on her other customers.

"In addition to Russ leaving, I've got Grady laid up with a broken leg so I'm short a stable hand," she said when her sister returned to the counter. "Do you think Simon's brother would be interested in a summer job again this year?"

Crystal tallied up a bill. "Ted's in Europe with his girlfriend for the next couple of months."

"Oh." Jewel pushed her now empty cup aside. "Know anyone else who might be interested?"

"Most of the local college kids already have their summer jobs lined up."

She sighed. "I guess I'll have to put an ad in the paper then."

"Sorry, I couldn't be more help," Crystal said. "I know how much you hate interviewing people."

"Actually the interviews don't concern me as much as the possibility that it might be too late to find qualified help for the summer."

"What kind of qualifications do you need to muck out stinky stalls?"

"Some experience working around animals would be helpful," she said dryly.

"What kind of animals?" a masculine voice asked from behind her.

She whirled around and found herself face-to-chest with the hunky stranger and couldn't help but notice how the polo shirt he wore stretched across impressive pectoral muscles. Cheeks hot, mouth dry, she lifted her gaze and found his eyes on her again.

Crystal offered profuse apologies as she refilled the cup in his hand.

"Not a problem," he assured her, then shifted his attention back to Jewel and asked again, "What kind of animals?"

She drew in a breath and, along with it, his scent. Clean and sharp and as tempting as the rest of him.

"Horses," she finally managed to respond to his question.

"Thoroughbred racehorses," Crystal elaborated. "My sister runs one of the top training facilities in the state."

Jewel's quelling glance was met with a sweet smile.

"I'm Mac Delgado," the man introduced himself. "I happen to know my way around horses and I'm looking for some short-term employment."

Jewel only said, "And I don't hire anyone without a rec-ommendation," and stepped away from the counter.

"I'll let you know if I find any suitable candidates," her sister called after her.

"Thanks, Crystal." She didn't turn back, but she knew he was watching her. She could feel the heat of his gaze on her as she made her way to the door.

He'd been dismissed—blatantly and unapologetically. It was a new experience for Mac Delgado—aka His Royal Highness Marcus Santiago, Prince of Tesoro del Mar—and not one he'd particularly enjoyed. She hadn't even given him her name, and he was frowning over that fact as he watched her walk out, enjoying the quick strides of long, lean legs and the subtle sway of slim hips until the door of the café swung shut behind her.

A soft sigh drew his attention back to the young waitress with the friendly smile. Crystal, the other woman had called her.

"She really doesn't mean to be rude," Crystal said now.

"And yet, she has such an obvious talent for it."

She smiled again, a little ruefully this time. "She's got a lot on her mind right now."

He shrugged, as if it didn't matter, as if he didn't have a hundred questions about the woman who'd walked out the door without so much as a backward glance in his direction. But he sat down on the stool she'd recently vacated as Crystal waved goodbye to an elderly couple as they headed out the door.

"So what brings you to Alliston?" she asked, turning her attention back to him.

"Road construction on the highway," he admitted.

She smiled at that. "Where are you headed?"

"California eventually."

"Driving?"

He nodded.

"You've got a long way to go."

"I'm not in a hurry," he told her.

"What's in California?" she asked. "Friends? A job? A wife?"

He fought the smile that tugged at his lips in response to her not-so-subtle probing. "None of the above."

"You have to give me more than that if you expect me to answer any questions about my sister."

"What makes you think I have any questions about your sister?"

She lifted a brow. "Then you aren't interested in seeing Jewel again?"

"Jewel?" he echoed, then realized it was her sister's name, and an apt description for the woman with wildly sexy hair and eyes the color of a summer sky before a storm.

And then there were her lips, glossy and full and as perfectly shaped as a cupid's bow. And her hair, miles of honey-gold corkscrew curls tumbled over her shoulders and down her back. And—

He caught a glimpse of Crystal's satisfied smile out of the corner of his eye and forced himself to sever the thought.

Her smile widened. "I believe you were telling me how much you weren't interested in my sister."

"Actually," he said, "you were going to tell me where I could find her."

Jewel was faxing her Help Wanted ad to the classifieds department at the local newspaper when the knock sounded at the door.

"Come in," she said, her eyes never lifting from the machine where she was manually inserting pages because it had a tendency to chew the paper if she used the automatic feeder. She'd been meaning to take the machine in for service, but kept forgetting. With so many other tasks to deal with on a daily basis, those that didn't directly impact the horses tended to get shifted to the bottom of the list and frequently forgotten.

The door creaked as it was pushed open, reminding her that oiling the hinges was another one of those tasks that she never seemed to get around to doing. On the other hand, she didn't have to worry about anyone sneaking up on her.

She fed the last page into the machine before turning around, and found herself looking at a pair of very broad shoulders—not covered in flannel or denim, as was usual around the stables, but a royal-blue polo shirt, complete with the embroidered logo of pony and rider on the left side. The shirt stretched over those shoulders, across a broad chest and tucked into a pair of belted jeans that fit nicely over narrow hips and long, muscular legs.

Her eyes shifted and discovered that the face was just as spectacular as the body, and not entirely unfamiliar.

It was the man from the café, and along with the sense of recognition came a quiver inside—a humming vibration that rippled from her center all the way to her fingertips and churned up everything in between. The sensation was both unexpected and unwelcome, and she fought against it as her gaze locked with his.

Amusement lurked in the depths of his dark eyes, as if he'd been aware of her perusal and wasn't bothered or surprised by it.

He was probably used to women ogling him—a man who looked that good would have to be—but that didn't excuse her own behavior. It had just been so long since Jewel had looked at a man and recognized him as such.

Around the stables, the men were her employees or customers, and over the past few years, she hadn't had much of a life beyond the stables. Her instinctive reaction to this man's arrival at the café had been proof of that. Her response now only reinforced that truth.

"Can I help you?" she asked, the politely neutral tone giving no hint of the hormones zinging around inside of her.

"Actually, I'm here to help you." His warm, rich voice was as sensual as a caress and caused another quiver of sensation deep in her belly.

She mentally cursed her sister, certain that Crystal was somehow responsible for this man's appearance here now.

"How do you think you can help me?" she asked cautiously.

"By taking the job you were talking about at the café."

She looked him over again—had, in truth, not been able to take her eyes off of him—and shook her head. While she didn't doubt that long, lean body was more than capable of the physical work she needed done, she did doubt that he'd ever done such physical labor. "I'm looking for someone to muck out stalls as well as groom and exercise my horses."

"That's what Crystal said," he agreed.

Yep—her sweet but interfering little sister's sticky fingerprints were all over this ambush.

"And you are?" she asked, vaguely recalling that he'd offered his name at the café but unable to remember what it was.

"Mac Delgado."

Her father had taught her that she could learn a lot about a man from his handshake, so she moved forward to take his proffered hand, undeniably curious about this one. His grip was firm, strong and the contact of his palm against hers sent an unexpected jolt of heat through her.

She saw a flicker of something in his eyes, as if he'd felt the jolt, too. Or maybe she was just imagining it. She disengaged her hand and lowered herself into the chair behind her desk. "I have to be honest, Mr. Delgado, you don't look much like a stable hand."

He shrugged. "I have a lot of experience with horses and I'm between jobs at the moment."

She eyed him skeptically but gestured to the chair across from her desk. "Tell me about your experience."

He sat, somehow owning the space rather than merely occupying it. There was an aura about him, a sense of command, as if he was accustomed to giving orders rather than taking them. It made her wonder again why he was really here, because she didn't believe it was to muck out her stalls.

"I assume you're asking about my experience with horses?" There was just the hint of a smile on his lips, and the gleam in those sinfully dark eyes suggested he was flirting with her.

She'd known guys like Mac Delgado before—guys who

trusted their good looks and easy charm to get them what they wanted in life, whatever that might be. Jewel wasn't going to fall for it, not this time, no matter how hard her heart pounded when he smiled at her.

Still, there was a part of her—a shallow, sex-deprived part—that was tempted to hire him just so she could have the pleasure of looking at him every day. Because she had no doubt that those muscles would ripple very nicely as he mucked out stalls—if he knew which end of a pitchfork to grab hold of. But hiring a man who obviously expected to get the job by offering little more than his name and a smile would be a mistake, and Jewel Callahan didn't make mistakes. Not anymore and especially not when it came to the business that carried her name.

"Yes, Mr. Delgado. I was asking about your relevant job experience."

He propped one foot onto the opposite knee, a casual pose that allowed her to picture him in Levi's and flannel, rather than the designer threads he was wearing. "I grew up around horses," he told her. "Even before I could walk, I was sitting on a pony."

"That doesn't prove you know the difference between a curry comb and a hoof pick," she noted.

He shrugged again, and she couldn't help but notice how his shirt moulded to the broad shoulders. "I've groomed more than a few horses, even helped train some of them."

"Do you have references?"

"Give me a trial period," he said. "A week to prove that I can do the job."

"No references," she concluded.

"I'm a hard worker."

"This is a busy stable—"

"Three days," he interrupted.

She shook her head with more than a little regret as she pushed her chair back from her desk. "I don't have the time or the patience to train anyone."

"Give me a chance—I promise you won't be disappointed."

"I might have been willing to give you that chance, if not for your hands."

His brows lifted. "What's wrong with my hands?"

"They lack the calluses of a man accustomed to physical labor."

"I've spent the last few years at school," he admitted. "But I wouldn't risk my life around animals who weigh more than six times as much as I do if I didn't know I wasn't capable."

She leaned back in her chair. "At school where?"

"If I give the right answer, do I get the job?"

"You're assuming there is a right answer."

His smile was filled with confidence and charm, and she felt a distinctly feminine flutter in her belly. "Isn't there?"

"No," she said. "And no about the job."

She might end up regretting her hasty decision if no one else responded to her ad, but she instinctively knew that hiring Mac Delgado would present a bigger risk than turning him away. Not just because his experience was unproven, but because of the way her heart raced whenever he was near.

Chapter Two

Four hours later, Marcus had checked out of his hotel and was retracing the route to Callahan Thoroughbred Center after Jewel had—reluctantly—reversed her decision about hiring him.

He wasn't sure he believed in fate, but he couldn't deny feeling that he'd been in the right place at the right time—first, when he'd walked into the café and noticed Jewel sitting at the counter, and again when a young stable hand rushed into her office to warn that an expectant mare was having trouble with her labor.

Not just any mare, as it turned out, but one Jewel had raised since it was a newborn filly, and she'd been frantic at the thought of losing both mother and baby.

With the vet more than an hour's drive away and most of her own personnel at the track in preparation for the next day's race, she'd had almost no choice but to trust Marcus's assurance that he could turn the breech foal. Of course, she'd given it her own best effort first, demonstrating more strength and stamina than he would have expected of a woman who was about five-feet-three-inches tall and hardly more than a hundred pounds. And only when her own efforts proved futile had she stepped aside for him.

He'd been sweating when he was done, not just because it was a messy and physically demanding task, but because he knew this was *his* only chance to convince *her* to give him a chance. He hadn't considered why it mattered or why the opinion of a woman he'd only just met meant anything to him, he only knew that it did.

Having been born royal, even if he had been the last of four sons, meant that he was accustomed to a certain amount of deference from the cradle. The wealth he'd inherited aside from his title ensured that he could live his life as he chose, while dictates of custom and tradition established the parameters within which he was expected to make those choices.

Now he was twenty-five years old and still didn't have a clue about what he really wanted to do with his life—except that at this point he wanted to know Jewel Callahan better. The woman in question, however, had made it clear that she only wanted a hired hand.

Of course, she didn't know who he was. He'd enrolled in school as Mac Delgado, trusting that the use of his mother's maiden name as his own would help him avoid media scrutiny and allow him to concentrate on his studies. And it had worked—more successfully even than he'd anticipated. In fact, soon after coming to America he'd realized few of his classmates could find Tesoro del Mar on a map. They certainly never suspected that Mac was a member of the royal family.

His anonymity hadn't made him any less sought after by the female coeds, confirming that his looks, charm and intelligence were almost as big a draw to members of the opposite sex in America as his royal status had been in Europe. And he found it interesting that the characteristics that had attracted so many women in the past were the same traits that made Jewel wary.

She was grateful to him—he was sure of that. Whether she felt anything beyond appreciation for his actions in delivering the foal he was less certain. But now that he'd been hired on, albeit on a trial basis, he would have some time to find out.

What he found, when he detoured to check on the new foal, was that the woman in question had the same idea.

She was standing at the gate, her arms folded on top of it, her attention riveted on the mare nursing her baby.

"Hard to believe she caused such a fuss only a few hours ago," Marcus noted.

"And scary to think how differently things might have turned out." She turned to face him. "I didn't expect you'd be back so soon."

"I didn't have a lot to pack," he told her.

But before he'd checked out of the hotel, he'd taken the time to shower and change, as he saw she had done, too.

Her jeans had been discarded in favor of a pair of khaki pants, the navy T-shirt replaced by a soft yellow one, and the band that tied her hair back had been removed so that the riotous golden curls tumbled over her shoulders.

She dug something out of her pocket, held it out to him. "The apartments aren't big or fancy, but they're conveniently located, a fact which you'll appreciate at 4:00 a.m. tomorrow morning."

He nodded and took the key she offered. "Thanks."

"There's a cafeteria on site, but also a refrigerator and microwave and some dishes and cutlery in your room."

He nodded again.

She tilted her head, and studied him as if he was a mystery she was trying to figure out. "When I told you I didn't think you were right for the job, I thought that would be the end of it."

"So did I," he admitted.

"Why did you follow me to the birthing shed?"

"Curiosity. Impulse." He lifted a shoulder. "I'm not entirely sure."

"Well, I'm grateful you did," she told him. "I could have lost both of them if you hadn't been here."

He touched a hand to her arm, to reassure her. When he felt the muscles go taut and heard her breath catch, he knew she was feeling more than just gratitude. Whether or not Jewel Callahan liked him, she wasn't immune to him.

He let his hand drop away and kept his voice light. "She's a beautiful filly."

"'The prettier they are, the more trouble they are.'"

His brows rose in silent inquiry.

"Jack Callahan's words of wisdom," she explained.

"I'm guessing you gave him a lot of trouble."

Her cheeks flushed in response to the compliment, but there was sadness lurking in the depths of those stormy blue-gray eyes as she shook her head. "Not really."

"Well, if I'd had to put money on it, I would have guessed the foal was a colt," he said.

"Why's that?"

"Because you said that she wasn't due for another couple

of weeks, and it's been my experience that females are rarely on time for anything, never mind early."

Her lips quirked at the corners, just a little. "I could pretend to take offense at that comment, except that I set my watch ten minutes ahead to help me get where I'm going on time."

It was the first insight she'd given him of her character, and while it wasn't a significant revelation, it was enough to give him hope that she might be warming up to him.

"Does it work?" he asked.

The smile nudged a little wider. "Usually."

The foal, her hunger now sated, curled up in the straw to sleep, and Scarlett moved to the feed bucket for her own dinner.

"Of course, the process of birth doesn't fit into any kind of schedule," he acknowledged.

"You obviously have some experience with that," she noted.

"I was eight years old the first time I saw a foal born."

And a few years after that, he'd witnessed a breech birth, and the complicated and time-consuming process of turning the foal. Even now, so many years later, he remembered the profound sadness that had washed through him when the roan filly was finally pulled free of her mother's womb. Even covered in what he'd referred to at the time as the slime of birth, he'd thought she was perfect and beautiful—and he'd known that her complete stillness was unnatural.

"You grew up on a farm?" she asked.

Her question drew him back to the present and made him want to smile. He'd never heard the royal palace described as such, but he supposed, in a way, it might be considered that. "The horses were more of a hobby than anything else."

"How many?"

"It varied. Sometimes half a dozen, sometimes more than twice that number."

"We have between eighty and a hundred here at any given time," she told him.

"I guess that means I'm going to be busy."

She nodded, her gaze drifting back to the mare and her foal. Another minute passed before she said, "This is a prestigious establishment. The races around here draw crowds from around the world and focus a lot of attention on Callahan. Two years ago, a former British prime minister was at the derby. Last year, it was the Princess Royal from some small country in the Mediterranean."

"You have a point, I'm guessing, other than name-dropping."

She nodded. "I can't afford to make mistakes where the business is concerned."

"You didn't make one in hiring me," he assured her.

"We agreed to a one-week trial period," she said. "If we're both satisfied with the way things are working out by the end of the week, we can discuss further terms."

"Then I'll look forward to our discussion at the end of the week."

"Cocky, aren't you?"

"Confident," he corrected, and smiled.

"In any event, I'm only looking for someone to fill in for a couple of months while Grady has a cast on his leg."

"Riding accident?"

"No. He tumbled off a ladder while taking down his Christmas lights."

"In May?"

Now she *really* smiled. "He didn't want to do it in January when it was icy and snowy because he might slip and fall."

She was even more beautiful when she smiled, when her eyes sparkled with humor and her lips tilted up at the corners. His gaze lingered on her mouth for a moment, wondering if it would taste as soft and moist as it looked, and certain that putting the moves on his new boss would be a good way to lose his job before he'd started.

He took a mental step back, because as attracted as he was to Jewel, he really did want this job.

He had three university degrees and countless royal duties waiting for him at home, but what appealed to him right now was the opportunity to work in these stables.

It was nothing less than the truth when he told Jewel he'd been riding since before he could walk. His father had taught all of his sons to ride, and with the duties of his office monopolizing so much of his time, the brothers had grown to appreciate those all-too-rare occasions when they'd raced across the hills together.

After his father's death, Marcus had started spending even more time in the stables, because it was there that he could recall his fondest and most vivid memories. It was when he was with the horses that he felt his father's presence most keenly. He hadn't realized how much he'd missed working with animals until this opportunity had come up and he wasn't going to blow it because of a woman—no matter how much she tempted him.

Still, he couldn't prevent his gaze from skimming over her again, couldn't help wondering if he'd ever seen eyes such an intriguing shade of gray-blue, if her hair was as silky as it looked, if the pulse fluttering at the base of her jaw would race if he brushed his fingertips over it.

He curled his fingers into his palms to resist the temptation to do just that.

* * *

Something had changed.

Jewel wasn't sure how or when, she only knew that it had.

One minute they were joking about Grady's clumsiness, then he was looking at her as if nothing existed but the both of them, as if there was no time except in that moment.

The very air around them seemed to be charged with an electricity that heightened her senses, amplified her awareness of him, magnified the needs that had been too long ignored.

She wasn't the type of woman whose knees went weak at the sight of an attractive man—at least, she never had been before. But that was precisely what had happened when she'd caught her first glimpse of Mac Delgado in the café.

He was a man who would make any woman look twice, so she didn't fault herself for doing so. Even her sister, who was unquestionably devoted to her husband, had sighed in appreciation when he'd walked in the door.

But he was also young—probably a decade younger than her—and she was old enough to recognize the dangers of getting involved with a man just because he was nice to look at.

Okay, he was a lot more than nice to look at, and he'd already proven that he was more than a pretty face. But she'd made the mistake of following her heart once before. She'd ignored her sister's concerns and her father's demands, and she'd let herself get swept away by her dreams. And she'd come home with those dreams and her heart shattered.

It was a mistake she wouldn't ever make again.

She pushed away from the gate. "I've got other animals to see to, and you need to get settled."

But as Jewel walked briskly from the barn, she felt anything but settled.

She'd meant what she said when she told him she couldn't afford to make mistakes with respect to the business. She was even less willing to take risks where her heart was concerned.

Though the idea of a casual affair held a certain and undeniable appeal, Jewel didn't dare let herself think about it. Because she'd never been able to share her body without first opening up her heart, and she had no intention of opening up her heart again.

You're too young to have resigned yourself to being alone.

Jewel tried to ignore the echo of her sister's words in her head, along with the admonition of her conscience that she'd lied to Crystal when she'd claimed she wasn't settling for less than what she wanted. Because the truth was, she wanted a husband, a family, a life outside of the farm where she'd grown up.

But while it wasn't entirely accurate to say that she was happy being alone, she was content. She'd become accustomed to quiet nights and an empty bed, accepting that was the price to be paid to protect her heart.

And if she sometimes desperately yearned for a baby of her own to hold in her arms, well, she'd just have to accept that wasn't going to happen for her—not without a ring on her finger first. And since she had no intention of falling in love again, she would just have to be satisfied with her role as doting aunt to any children her sister might have.

As for Mac Delgado, she was probably misinterpreting her feelings for him because she was grateful for his help in delivering Scarlett's foal, exaggerating the attraction because it had been so long since she'd been with a man.

She frowned, trying to figure out exactly how long it had been, then realized if she had to think about it that hard, she probably didn't want to know.

* * *

When Jewel left the stables, she saw that Russ had returned from his errands in town, and her lips curved with genuine pleasure as she made her way toward him. Her smile slipped a little when she noted the scowl that darkened his usually handsome face.

"Did you see Scarlett's foal?" she asked.

His only response was an abrupt nod. Then he jerked his head in the direction of the barn. "Was that him?"

"Who?"

"The guy who drove up in the fancy wheels. Is he the new groom Cody said you hired?"

She nodded. "Mac Delgado."

His scowl deepened. "What do you know about him, JC?"

"I know that he doesn't panic under pressure."

"You hired him because he helped deliver a foal?"

"It's not my usual interview technique, but I'd say he more than proved himself. If he hadn't been here, I might have lost both Scarlett and the baby."

"Cody would have come through for you."

"Cody was shaking so badly I'm surprised he managed to dial the phone when I asked him to call the vet."

"You're mad that I wasn't here."

She shook her head. "There's no point in being angry about anything. There weren't any of the usual indicators that she was going to foal so soon and, truthfully, if she'd waited another couple of weeks, you'd be gone anyway."

"Is that why you hired the first guy who showed up here?"

She shifted her gaze away, not willing to admit that she still had her own reservations about Mac—though they were more personal than professional. And considering the way he'd come through for her, she figured she owed him a chance. "I don't answer to you, Russ."

"No," he acknowledged. "But it used to be we talked about things, made decisions together."

"That was before you decided to leave."

"Are you going to throw that up at me in every single conversation we have over the next nine days?"

"Maybe."

His jaw tightened.

She sighed. "I'm sorry, Russ. I know that wasn't fair."

"I'm not abandoning you, Jewel." The quiet words were filled with understanding.

She nodded, grateful that he didn't say what they were both thinking. Like her mother. Like Thomas and Allan and everyone else who had ever claimed to love her. And she knew he honestly didn't see his leaving as yet another abandonment—but it sure felt that way to Jewel.

Marcus worked closely with Russ over the next seven days, learning the routines of the farm and getting acquainted with the animals and the people who worked with them. He barely crossed paths with Jewel during that time and she certainly never stopped to engage him in conversation. In fact, the most response he ever got from her was a nod acknowledging his presence—certainly no more than any other employee.

At first, he enjoyed the novelty of being treated just like the other men. But after a few days, her indifference started to frustrate rather than amuse him. Until he realized it was *studied* indifference—and that she would only have to make such a deliberate effort to ignore him if she was as aware of his presence as he was of hers.

He heard her name come up in conversations and blatantly eavesdropped, trying to piece together a picture of who the woman referred to by most of her employees as "JC" really was. He was surprised to learn that she'd spent some time on the rodeo circuit before her father's first heart attack several years earlier, after which she had come home to help with the running of the facility. He also learned that she was both liked and respected by the men in her employ, most of whom had been with the Callahan Thoroughbred Center for years.

The owners who came to the onsite track to monitor the progress of their horses weren't as unanimous in their praise. While they thoroughly approved of the facility, they weren't sure that "Jack's daughter"—as Jewel was frequently labeled—had her daddy's head for business. And then they'd look across the fields and shake their heads. Mac had yet to figure out what that was all about.

By the end of the week, he was exhausted. But it was a good exhaustion—the kind that came from hard physical work. His hands weren't as soft as they'd been the first day he came to the farm, but the sting of blisters was a small price to pay for the enjoyment of working with the horses and the satisfaction of knowing he'd done a good job.

"Hey, Mac." Crystal tossed him an easy smile and a quick wave as she passed by the track, where he was watching some of the yearlings work out.

"Hi, Crystal. Where are you racing off to?" he asked, falling into step beside her.

"Haven. And I'm late."

"Where's Haven?"

She stopped in her tracks and stared at him. "How long have you been working here?"

"My seven-day trial period ended today. Since your sister hasn't fired me yet, I assume she's willing to keep me on."

"I can't believe she hasn't told you about Haven," Crystal said, picking up her pace again. "She never misses an opportunity to rope someone into helping out, if she can."

"Helping out with?" he prompted

She stopped outside of a barn that was on the far side of CTC's property. He'd noticed the building before, but because it was so distant from the hub of CTC, he'd assumed it was owned by someone else. There was a brass oval on the door with the silhouette of a horse's head inside it and the word "Haven" spelled out in brass letters above it.

"This is Haven," she told him.

He followed her inside, immediately noting that it was as clean and organized as any of the buildings at CTC if somewhat more utilitarian in design. The floor was concrete rather than cobblestone and the names of the stalls' residents noted on white boards rather than engraved on brass plates, but the stalls were still twelve-by-twelve and filled with straw bedding.

"Jewel started Haven for old or injured racehorses. The big money winners are well taken care by their owners, but those with less successful careers are sometimes neglected and often resented because of the high cost of their maintenance. Those unwanted animals come here until she can find them new homes."

A huge draft horse tossed his head over the stall door and whinnied.

"That isn't a thoroughbred," he said.

"No," Crystal agreed. "Some of them are, some aren't. But they're all horses that have been rescued or are in need of rehabilitation."

"So this is what she does in her spare time," he murmured.

"Jack Callahan established the Center," Crystal told him. "Jewel took over running it after he died because she could, and because she loves horses. But CTC is a business. This is her passion.

"And this—" she indicated a powerfully built chestnut in the end stall "—is Cayenne. Also known as The Demon Stallion."

"Temperamental?" he guessed.

"You might say," Crystal agreed. "His trainer thought a heavy hand with the crop would teach him to obey. Instead it taught him to be mean. And then there was an incident in the stables and—" She shook her head. "Let's just say his owners wrote him off."

Marcus had heard about trainers like that and thought the crop should be used on them. How anyone could abuse such a beautiful animal—or any creature—was beyond him. And while he didn't doubt Cayenne was capable of acting like a demon, right now the horse just looked wary, and scared.

He moved closer, keeping one eye on the stallion and his voice low. "How did he end up here?"

"Jewel heard about him from a friend of a friend, or something like that. It's hard to keep all of their stories straight sometimes."

He was starting to realize there was a lot more to the story of Jewel Callahan than she wanted him to know.

"Anyway," Crystal continued, "the owner was looking to unload him rather than invest in further training, so Jewel made him an offer. Now she's faced with the challenge of undoing the damage that has been done so that she can find a good home for him."

"Who decides what a good home is?" Mac asked.

"Jewel, of course. But never before a personal interview with the potential buyer and a thorough inspection of the premises."

"Is there anything she doesn't do?" he wondered aloud.

Crystal grinned. "She doesn't make a cheesecake that compares to mine."

"I have a weakness for cheesecake," Mac admitted.

And he had a growing fascination with Jewel Callahan. The more he knew about the beautiful, stubborn woman who had reluctantly given him a job, the more he wanted to know. And he had a pretty good idea about how to get what he wanted.

Cayenne was in the paddock when Jewel returned to the farm after her trip into town, so she knew her sister was cleaning his stall. Knowing how much Crystal hated that job, she felt a twinge of guilt that she'd been gone as long as she had, but only a slight twinge. Crystal had been helping out at Haven since they took in their first horse, but with her own business turning into such a success, she'd had to severely cut back her volunteer time. Since she was only able to put in a few hours on Tuesdays and Fridays now, Jewel figured mucking out a couple of stalls was actually necessary to keep her in practice.

But as she carried the bags of vitamin supplements through to the storeroom, she couldn't resist teasing. "You must be losing your touch, Crys, if you didn't manage to sweet-talk some cute stable hand into doing that for you."

But the head that popped up in response to her comment was neither blond nor female, and "cute" was far too bland a description to do it justice.

"Hey," Mac said.

"Obviously she hasn't lost her touch," Jewel muttered beneath her breath.

But not so quietly that Mac didn't hear, because he flashed her an easy grin that, even from a distance of twenty-five feet, made her tummy quiver.

"Does that mean you think I'm cute?" he asked.

She ignored the question. "You haven't mucked out enough stalls already this week?"

"More than enough," he assured her, leaning on the handle of the pitchfork.

"Where is my sister?" Jewel asked. "And how did she con you into doing her job?"

"She didn't con me—she bribed me."

"With?"

"Promises of homemade cherry cheesecake."

Jewel began stacking bottles and jars on the appropriate shelves. "I'd say she got the better end of the deal, but she does make a spectacular cheesecake."

"Pot roast was also mentioned," he told her.

"Crystal invited you up to the house for dinner?" Not that she objected, exactly. And since Simon had a late meeting and Crystal would be dining with them, she had no reason to object. But she was still a little wary of her sister's reasons for issuing the invitation.

"She thought it would give you and I an opportunity to talk about my duties for the next several weeks."

"If you want to stay on, I'd be happy to have you continue doing what you've been doing."

"I want to stay on," he told her. "And I want to help out here."

She closed and latched the door. "Why?"

"Because it's obvious to me that you could use a couple extra hands."

"I could use a dozen extra hands," she admitted. "But

Haven doesn't have the funds to hire any help. Mostly we take on coop students from the local high school."

"And you come in every day after they're finished to redo what wasn't done properly," he guessed, tossing fresh bedding into the stall.

She shrugged. "They're kids. They do the best they can."

"And they're scared to death of Cayenne."

"There's no shame in being afraid of a twelve-hundred-pound animal. Randy Porter trained horses for more than thirty-five years and even he watches his step around Cayenne."

Mac finished spreading the straw before he turned to her. "I could work with him."

She'd have to be crazy to let him. He'd proven he was a competent groom, but what he was suggesting was way beyond the scope of anything he'd been doing in the past week, and Cayenne wasn't like any of the horses he'd encountered at CTC. The Demon Stallion had earned his nickname by being both difficult and unpredictable, and though Jewel had been working with him personally over the past couple of months, she'd made little progress.

But while she might worry about Cayenne's inconsistent behavior, her own had been no better. When she'd started training him, she'd planned to spend a couple of hours with him every day. The reality was that she didn't always have a couple of hours to spare, there were simply too many demands on her to be able to dedicate the time and attention he needed.

And there were too many reasons why she should refuse Mac's offer, not the least of which was that if he started hanging out around the Haven stable, their paths would cross more often.

On the other hand, if she spent enough time around Mac

she might become inured to his presence so that warm tingles didn't dance through her veins every time he looked at her, and her heart didn't skip a beat every time he smiled.

"Dinner's at six," she finally said. "We can talk about it then."

Chapter Three

Jewel decided to grab a quick shower after she finished up at Haven and was just tugging on a clean pair of jeans when she heard a knock on the back door. A quick glance at the clock confirmed that it was almost six. Confident that the housekeeper would let him in, she didn't hurry. She was combing her fingers through the unruly mass of hair she'd released from its ponytail when the knock came again.

Ignoring the socks she'd tossed on the bed, she made her way to the kitchen. Where she expected to find Bonnie hovering at the stove, she instead found a note.

Crystal is driving me into town to pick up a package at FedEx. Dinner is in the oven. Enjoy.

She noted the two place settings along with the candles and wine on the table and seriously doubted that there was any package. She'd invited Mac to dinner because she'd believed

Crystal and Bonnie would also be there. But somehow her conniving sister had managed to take what was supposed to be a business discussion over a meal and made it look like a date. And while she understood her sister's motivations, she had no intention of being manipulated.

She tucked the candles and wine into the pantry, returned the stemware to the cupboard and moved the place settings to opposite ends of the table before she went to answer the door.

The first thing Mac noticed when Jewel opened the door was that she'd showered and changed since she'd left the stable. Her hair tumbled freely down her back, her freshly scrubbed skin glowed and her feet were bare. She wasn't wearing any makeup that he could tell, but she looked beautiful, natural.

She noticed the flowers in his hand and frowned. "You shouldn't have brought me flowers."

"They're only for you if you cooked the pot roast." He was pleased to note that his response had surprised her, because he suspected that the only way he was going to make progress with Jewel was to give her the unexpected and keep her off her stride.

"I didn't." She smiled wryly. "For which we should both be truly grateful."

He smiled back. "Then the daisies are for Bonnie."

"You've met Bonnie?"

"Not yet, but your sister did such a good job extolling her culinary virtues I almost feel as if I have."

"Well, you won't meet her tonight, either. She had an errand to run in town." Jewel took the flowers from him. "But I'll put these in water for her and tell you that she'd appreciate the thought."

As he followed her into the house, he thought *she* smelled good enough to eat, though he didn't think the citrusy scent was perfume. She didn't seem the type to bother with such frills. More likely the scent was from some kind of lotion or cream that she'd rubbed onto her skin after her shower.

He firmly shoved *that* tempting image from his mind and glanced around the kitchen.

The table and chairs appeared to be solidly built and obviously well used. The dishes were stoneware rather than china, the cutlery was stainless instead of silver, the napkins made of paper not linen. It was a family table, and the rich aromas that filled the air were those of a good, home-cooked meal, and he found the simplicity of everything appealed to him.

As Jewel appealed to him.

Noting that the table was set for two, he said, "I thought your sister would be here for dinner."

"So did I."

Something in her tone suggested that she wasn't only surprised—but annoyed—by Crystal's change of plans. And he wondered if it was the thought of dining alone with him that bothered her.

"Does her absence mean there's no cheesecake?" he asked.

"No." She smiled as she carried a tray laden with thick slices of beef and chunky roasted vegetables to the table. "The cheesecake's in the fridge."

"Well, that's a relief," he said.

She gestured for him to sit, but he scooped the basket of warm rolls and the pitcher of steaming gravy from the counter to set on the table before she could do so.

She slanted him a look, as if his willingness to assist with domestic chores was something else she hadn't expected, but silently took her own seat on the other side of the table.

He loaded his plate with a generous helping of beef and vegetables and noted that she did the same. When he passed her the pitcher of gravy, she smothered her plate with it.

They chatted casually while they ate, about the horses and the routines in her stables and then about thoroughbred training and racing in general. He enjoyed her company as much as dinner because of her sharp intelligence and wry humor and found he was reluctant for the meal to end.

When she got up to get dessert, she frowned at the clock. "Is it seven-thirty already?"

"Looks like," he agreed. "Is there somewhere else you need to be?"

"No." She slid a generous slice of cake onto a plate. "I was just wondering what kind of errand could have kept Bonnie out so long."

As if on cue, the phone rang. Jewel passed him the plate then excused herself to answer the call.

"That was Bonnie checking in," she said, when she returned to the table. "Apparently she and Crystal decided to stop for coffee and got caught up chatting with some mutual acquaintance."

He stabbed his fork into the cake, noting that while she'd started to relax over dinner, she wasn't so relaxed now. Was she anxious for him to leave? Or nervous because the phone call had reminded her that they were alone together?

She sat back down with obvious reluctance and cut herself a much smaller piece of cake.

"Tell me about Haven," he said. "The more I know about it, the more useful I can be."

"Why are you so eager to help out?"

"I figured that was obvious," he said. "I'm trying to ingratiate myself to you so you'll keep me around, maybe even consider having a hot and torrid affair with me."

Jewel glanced at Mac across the table. "Was that comment intended to fluster or flatter me?"

He shrugged. "I'm guessing it failed on both counts."

Actually it had succeeded on both counts, but she wasn't willing to let him know it. Or know that she'd given some thought to the same thing.

"Are you always so suspicious when someone offers you help?" he asked her.

"Let's just say that I've learned to look for the strings that are usually attached."

"I like horses," he said. "And, for some reason, I like you, too. Maybe it did occur to me that spending time at Haven might result in spending time with you, but my motives are no more nefarious than that."

"Well, you were right about extra hands being needed at Haven," she said. "And if you really want to spend your spare time there, I have no objection."

"That's incredibly gracious of you," he said.

She smiled at his dry tone. "Yeah, Crystal's always telling me I need to work on my social skills. But the horses don't usually complain."

"I'm not complaining," he said.

She took the tray of leftovers to the counter to wrap up. She heard the scrape of chair legs on the floor as Mac pushed away from the table, too, then brought their plates to the counter.

"Are you going to question my motives for clearing the table, too?"

She bit down on her lip, because she'd been tempted to do exactly like that. Instead she said, "I appreciate your help, but I can handle it."

He ignored her and began loading the dishwasher.

"You've got to be up early in the morning," she pointed out.

"And you'll be up just as early," he noted. "Whatever time I walk into the stable, you've already been there."

"It's my stable," she pointed out.

"No one's disputing that." He nudged her aside with his hip so he could move around to the other side of the dishwasher.

The brief contact shot arrows of awareness zinging through her system.

She stepped back quickly and braced her hands on the counter behind her. As she did so, her elbow bumped a water goblet on the counter and sent it crashing to the floor. The glass shattered, jagged shards flying.

Silently cursing her clumsiness, she started toward the closet for the broom.

"Watch," Mac said.

"I am," she snapped irritably, then swore when she stepped down on a piece of glass.

She lifted her foot, saw the blood was already dripping.

Before she could say anything, he scooped her up off her feet and lifted her onto the counter. Her breath whooshed out of her, though she wasn't sure if that was because of the un-expected jolt when he plunked her down or the surprising thrill of being held by a strong man.

He took a step back and picked up her foot. His hand was warm, his touch firm but gentle, and somehow incredibly sensual.

"Mac—"

He snagged a paper towel from the roll. "Just let me take a look."

She didn't see as she had much choice in the matter. And when his thumb slid over her instep, she didn't protest because she was incapable of speaking.

He dabbed gently at the blood. "You up-to-date on your tetanus shots?"

"I had one a couple of years ago," she said.

"It doesn't look like it needs a stitch, but it definitely needs some antiseptic cream and a bandage."

"There's a first-aid kit in the bathroom. If you let me get down, I'll—"

"You stay put," he said. "I'll get it."

"You give orders better than you take them, Mac," she noted when he returned with the box of medical supplies.

He shrugged. "I didn't figure you wanted to get blood all over the floor by hobbling around before that cut was tended to."

She didn't, of course, but that wasn't the point. "I would have managed just fine if you weren't here."

In fact, she probably wouldn't have knocked the glass off the counter if he hadn't been there to distract her—not that she was going to admit as much to him.

She sucked in a breath when he wiped an antiseptic pad over the bottom of her foot.

"You're being ungrateful again," he told her.

She frowned at that. "I'm used to doing things on my own."

"Then it's not just me," he noted, dabbing some cream onto the pad of a Band-Aid before affixing it to her wound.

"No."

His fingers smoothed down the edges of the dressing,

and caused those tingles to dance and swirl through her system again.

"Maybe," she muttered under her breath.

Not quietly enough, obviously, because he looked up at her and grinned.

"That should take care of it," he said, finally releasing her foot.

But he didn't move away, and she was suddenly aware of the intimacy of their positions—of the cupboards behind her back, and the man standing between her thighs.

"I need to, uh, get that glass swept up."

He stayed where he was, his hands on the counter, bracketing her knees. "Are you always this skittish when anyone gets too close?"

She laid her hands on his chest and tried not to think about the solid muscles beneath her palms, the strong beat of his heart, or the heat of his skin as she pushed him back a few inches.

The intensity in his gaze made everything inside her quiver, but she managed to keep her eyes level with his and her voice steady when she responded. "I have this thing about personal space—as in, I don't like people in mine."

Before he could say anything else, a flash of headlights warned of a vehicle coming up the driveway.

"That will be Crystal dropping Bonnie off," she told him, torn between relief and disappointment that their time alone together was about to be interrupted. Because as much as she did tend to veer away from intimacy, she occasionally experienced pangs of loneliness, moments when she was sometimes even tempted to open up her heart again. Usually those moments were quick to pass and her life would go back to normal.

But Mac Delgado had shaken up the status quo the minute

he walked into the Halfway Café, and Jewel didn't know what—if anything—she was going to do about him.

Mac's knowing expression suggested that he'd picked up on her mixed emotions, that he knew how confused she was and how tempted she didn't want to be. She found it strange that a man she'd met only a week earlier should be able to see through all the layers she'd worked so hard to build up over the years and recognize the longing that was buried deep in her heart.

And she knew that if she wasn't careful, he might find a way to tunnel through those layers.

As Mac found the broom and quickly swept up and disposed of the broken glass, Jewel promised herself that she would be careful. Very careful.

Jewel was making some adjustments to the yearling training schedule on her computer when Caleb Bryant came into her office. He'd started as an exercise boy for her father when Jewel was still riding ponies and they'd grown up and into the business together. Now he wasn't just an Eclipse-winning trainer but a good friend.

The ready smile faded when she saw the concern etched between his dark brows.

"Gabe Anderson was here," he told her.

It was all he said, and yet those few words said so much. Gabe Anderson had been a client of Callahan for a long time, and he'd never made any secret of the fact that he had doubts about JC's ability to run the facility as her father had done. Jewel would have liked to be able to tell him to take his horses elsewhere, but the fact was, he had a fair amount of clout in the racing world and a lot of horseflesh in her stables. So she gritted her teeth and tried to accommodate his needs and wishes whenever possible, but something in Caleb's eyes warned it wouldn't be so easy this time.

"Is there a problem?"

"After Midnight came ninth in a field of fourteen at Belmont on the weekend."

She rubbed at the throb in her temple. The headache had been hovering there for a couple of hours, but she'd managed to stave it off with a handful of aspirin and focused determination. Until now.

"Should he have done better?"

Caleb only shrugged. "He's a young colt with a lot of potential, but right now, he has more enthusiasm than focus."

And that was the reason, she suspected, that Caleb had recommended not racing the colt so early in the season. The two-year-old had been a late season foal and would have benefited from a few more months training before being loaded into a starting gate. But he was also a foal with impressive bloodlines and a price tag to match, and she knew that Anderson was focused so intently on seeing a return for his investment that he couldn't see anything else.

"I just wanted to let you know that he's blustering," Caleb said. "About the possibility of taking his horses elsewhere—as he threatens to do at least once a year, or—and this is a new one to me—maybe building his own stables."

She nodded, and wished she hadn't when her pounding head protested the motion. "I appreciate the heads-up."

He turned to leave, pausing in the doorway to say, "We both know he won't find another facility in the state that compares to this one."

She managed a smile. "Or a trainer like the one here."

Caleb smiled back. "Well, that goes without saying."

After he'd gone, Jewel thought about the training schedule she had yet to finish, and decided it could wait. She wasn't going to sort anything out while her head was pounding.

"Dinner will be ready in a few minutes," Bonnie said when she tugged off her boots inside the back door.

"I'm not really hungry," Jewel said.

"You didn't come in for lunch, so unless you have a kitchen in your office that I don't know about, you haven't eaten since breakfast."

"I had a chocolate bar and a Diet Coke."

"Which would explain the headache."

"Which is why I just want a bath and bed."

Bonnie's lips thinned. "You've forgotten."

Jewel winced, because obviously she had, though even now, she couldn't remember what it was that she'd forgotten.

"The boys are giving Russ his big send-off at The Mustang tonight," the housekeeper reminded her.

Jewel wasn't sure if she'd forgotten or deliberately put it out of her mind, because to think about the party was to think about Russ leaving, and that was still too painful. "I'm not up to going out tonight."

"You most certainly are going." Bonnie folded her arms across her chest in a posture that clearly communicated the matter wasn't open for debate.

She had been Jack Callahan's housekeeper since long before he married Jewel's mother, and when Lorraine Callahan ran out on her husband and daughter, Bonnie had taken over the day-to-day care of the child Jack had shown even less interest in than had the woman who'd left her behind. She was so much more than an employee to Jewel—

she was a mother figure, a role model and a trusted friend, and she never hesitated to speak what was on her mind.

"Now take something for your headache and go have that bath before dinner," she continued. "You'll feel better then and you won't have to spend the next six months wallowing in guilt and regret that you didn't take the time to say goodbye to your best friend."

Jewel wanted to resent the housekeeper's high-handedness, but the truth was, she was right. And after she'd popped a couple of Tylenol, soaked in the tub for half an hour and had a quick bite, she was feeling better. Maybe not quite looking forward to a night on the town but accepting of the fact that she needed to make an appearance.

And then she walked out to her truck and found Mac waiting for her.

She'd caught glimpses of him now and again around both the CTC stables and at Haven, though she'd taken care to ensure that their paths didn't cross any more than was absolutely necessary. She'd needed the distance to figure out the feelings he'd stirred inside of her, and had almost managed to convince herself that the warm, tingly feeling she got when he looked at her was just gratitude tangled up with the joy and relief that Scarlett's foal had been delivered safely.

But a week and a half had passed since then and nothing had changed. He was looking at her now, and that warm, tingly feeling was back, and she feared the explanation wasn't that simple. It wasn't gratitude she was feeling but attraction.

And the dark glint in his eyes told her that he was feeling the same thing.

When she'd dressed, she hadn't known that Mac would be there. The possibility had crossed her mind, of course, as thoughts of him had crossed her mind all too frequently over the past several days, but she hadn't been certain. She'd pretended that she didn't care one way or the other, but she found herself taking extra care with her appearance anyway. Nothing too obvious, just a touch of mascara to darken her lashes, a swipe of gloss over her lips, a spritz of perfume that had rarely been taken out of the box.

But as his eyes moved over her, his lips curving in a slow smile of obvious appreciation, she was glad she'd made the effort—and still more than a little wary about the tingly feeling inside.

"What are you doing here, Mac?"

"I was hoping to ride into town with you."

"What's wrong with your Navigator?"

"Nothing. I just thought it made sense to carpool, since we're both going the same way."

"Did my sister put you up to this?"

He ignored her question, asking instead, "So what do you say—can I hitch a ride?"

The last thing she wanted was to be trapped in the cab of her truck with a man whose mere proximity put every one of her nerve endings on high alert. Unfortunately, she had no valid reason to refuse his request, not when they were both heading in the same direction. After a moment, she finally shook her head.

"No—" she tossed him the keys "—you can drive."

Chapter Four

Jewel didn't worry about any speculation that might result from her showing up at the Mustang with Mac. The men she worked with knew her well enough to know that she wouldn't get personally involved with an employee, though in the close confines of the truck's cab on the way to the bar, she'd had to consciously remind herself of the same thing.

Limiting their interactions over the past week and a half had done nothing to lessen her response to him, but she knew that maintaining a physical distance was necessary if she was going to keep a clear head and continue to resist the attraction that seemed to be drawing them inevitably closer together.

She excused herself and slipped away from him as soon as they entered the bar, and he let her go without protest, making her question that conclusion. As she wandered through the crowd, exchanging greetings with familiar faces, she had to wonder if the attraction she felt wasn't reciprocated. Maybe the only hormones running riot were her own.

"If you don't stop frowning, the guest of honor might think you're not having a good time."

She turned to smile at Russ. "My mind was wandering."

"Apparently." He was carrying two glasses of beer, handed one to her. "You missed your sister. She and Simon stopped in for a quick goodbye."

"I'm glad she was able to make it." She followed him to a table in the corner.

"Then you're not still mad at her for not marrying me?"

Jewel rolled her eyes. "Is there any part of our conversation she didn't share with you?"

"Probably not," he said.

They chatted a little more, about the farm and Riley's tour, ordered another round of drinks.

"You haven't asked about Mac," he noted.

"Was I supposed to?"

"I figured you'd want to know how he was working out."

"And I figured if there was a problem, I would have heard about it before now."

He nodded at that. "He catches on fast, isn't afraid to get his hands dirty and gets along well with the other guys."

"Why do I hear a 'but' in your voice?"

"Because there's just something about him that I still can't figure out."

She glanced over her shoulder, saw that Mac was looking at her, and felt the tingles of awareness skate all the way down her spine.

She'd had lovers. True, she could count the number on one hand, but she wasn't completely inexperienced. But she had never experienced the instant tug of attraction she felt when her eyes had locked with his the very first time. A tug that had only become more insistent with each passing day.

"Everyone has secrets." She turned back to Russ, unwilling to admit she'd spent too much time trying—and failing—to figure out Mac Delgado. "All that matters is that he's capable of doing the job he was hired to do."

"Then your interest in him isn't at all personal?"

"You *have* been talking to my sister."

"I already told you I was," he said. "But I also have eyes in my head."

"Those must come in handy when you need to get back from way out in left field."

He grinned. "You're forgetting that I've known you for a long time."

"Then you should know me well enough to know that I would never jeopardize a professional association by getting involved in a personal relationship."

"Never say never," Russ warned.

Marcus wasn't worried about the fact that Jewel was cozied up in the corner with Russ Granger. He might have wondered about their relationship when she first hired him on, about the easy camaraderie they shared and their obvious rapport, but over the past week and a half, he'd realized their closeness was friendly rather than romantic. A definite relief to him since he'd decided that he wanted Jewel in his bed and her potential involvement with someone else would be a major obstacle to those plans. His playboy reputation aside, he'd never let himself get tangled up with a woman who was otherwise engaged. Not knowingly, anyway.

Still, the fact that Jewel didn't share an intimate relationship with Granger didn't mean she *wasn't* involved with someone else. And when the other man finally said goodbye and walked away, he decided it was time to stop wondering.

He ordered another draft for Jewel and a Coke for himself, then slid into the now vacant seat across from her.

"It just occurred to me," he said, "that this is my first Alliston nightlife experience."

"Has it been memorable?" she asked.

"It has potential."

"If you want nightlife, you won't find much of it here," she told him. "There are a couple of restaurants in town, this bar, a movie theater and a bowling alley."

He sipped his Coke. "If I wanted to take a woman on a date, where would you suggest I take her?"

"Charleston," Jewel responded without hesitation.

"You want to go to Charleston with me sometime?"

She shook her head without a hint of reluctance or any hesitation.

"It's okay if you need to think about it or want to check your calendar," he told her.

"I don't need to think about it or check my calendar, because I'm not going on a date with you, Mac."

"You might have at least made an effort to let me down easy."

"Have I dented your pride?"

"Inflicted a mortal wound," he said solemnly.

"Somehow I doubt that."

"Are you involved with someone?"

"No." She picked up her glass, sipped her draft. "Nor am I looking to complicate my life with any personal involvements right now."

"My father once told me that it's only when we stop looking that we find our heart's desire."

Her lips curved, offering him just a hint of a smile that made him want to see more.

"Sounds like he's either a philosopher or a romantic," she said.

"He was a lot of things," Mac said. "Mostly a good man and a great father who was taken away from his family far too soon."

"How long ago was that?" she asked gently.

"Almost eight years."

"It must have been difficult, losing him when you were so young."

He smiled at that, as he realized she was trying to gauge exactly how old he was. Because she was interested? Or just curious?

"How young do you figure I was?" he countered.

"Fourteen?"

"Actually I was seventeen."

"And you said you just finished school," she said, considering. "So you must have taken some time off before college, goofed off in college, or you have more than one degree."

"Something like that."

"You never did tell me where you went to school."

Damn—he should have seen that question coming. But he only shrugged and answered, "Harvard."

Her brows arched. "Definitely not a goof-off."

The last pounding notes of an AC/DC song that had been playing on the jukebox faded out and an Aerosmith ballad took its place.

"Dance with me," he said, pushing away from the table and offering his hand.

She shook her head. "I can't."

"Can't dance?"

"I can't dance with you," she said.

"Because—" he prompted.

"Because this bar is filled with people both of us work with nd—"

"Actually almost everyone else is gone."

She glanced around in surprise, then at her watch. "Oh, my oodness. I had no idea it had gotten to be so late." Then she oked up at him. "Why didn't you catch a ride back with meone else?"

"Going home to a cold, empty bed or enjoying the mpany of a warm, beautiful woman—" he grinned "—it emed an obvious choice to me."

Jewel was flattered—how could she not be? But she also new that it was important to set some boundaries between em. No doubt he was aware of her attraction to him, but she eded to let him know that she had no intention of acting on at attraction, no matter how tempted she might be.

"Look, Mac—"

"It's just a dance, Jewel."

She wasn't sure that was true, but when he took her hand, e forgot all of her protests and let him lead her to the tiny ance floor. There were only two other couples dancing, other with their heads close together in the corner and a ndful of men lingering at the bar. It was a Thursday night, ter all, and morning came early in a town that had been built ound the thoroughbred racing industry.

It's just a dance, she reminded herself as Mac turned her his arms.

And yet, dancing with him was like something out of a ntasy. He had an innate grace for someone so big and strong, and though he pulled her close, he didn't hold her so tight that their bodies were pressed together like those of the other couples on the dance floor. Just close enough so that their thighs brushed as they moved, close enough that she could smell the heady masculine scent of him, close enough that her own body was starting to melt from the heat of his.

In the short time he'd been employed at the farm, he'd been working hard, as evidenced by the calluses that had already started to build up. The hardness of the skin on his palms made her think about the delicious sensation of those work-roughened hands moving over her naked body, and she had to keep her face averted so he wouldn't see her flushed cheeks.

She was so caught up in the erotic fantasy that she stumbled on the next step. He shifted easily, so that the miscue was hardly noticeable. Except that he was holding her closer now, so that the tips of her breasts rubbed against the solid wall of his chest, and her nipples hardened in instinctive response to the delicious friction.

Did he know? Could he tell how aroused she was becoming? She was mortified to think that he could—until she realized that certain parts of his body had responded to the contact, too. Apparently she wasn't the only one who was aroused.

Though the realization set every nerve ending in her body on fire and made her want to press herself tight against him, she managed to resist, all too aware that giving into such impulses would result in her getting burned.

Jewel breathed an almost audible sigh of relief when the song finally ended. She moved out of his arms, determined to keep her own desires under control—and Mac at a safe distance.

* * *

It took more willpower than Marcus would have thought to leave Jewel at her door and walk away without giving in to the temptation to kiss her. She'd looked so damn beautiful in the moonlight, and when her head had tipped back and his gaze had dropped to her lips—

Mi Dios, the woman had a mouth that was made to be kissed.

Her lips were full and soft, and when the tip of her tongue had swept over her lips, leaving them glistening with moisture, it had been all he could do not to haul her into his arms and cover that delectable mouth with his own.

She would have kissed him back—he had no doubts about that. When he'd held her in his arms on the dance floor, he'd felt the beat of her heart against his own. When he'd looked at her, he'd seen the awareness and desire that stirred in his own blood. Yes, she would have kissed him back. And then she would have kicked him out on his butt.

He smiled wryly at that thought as he walked to his rooms over the stables. It would have been just the excuse she needed to get rid of him, to push him away and pretend she didn't want him as much as he wanted her. And though he suspected that one kiss from Jewel Callahan would be worth it, he knew it would be a mistake to push for too much too soon. For now, he would simply have to be content himself with contemplating the possibilities.

Had he ever been so preoccupied with thoughts of a woman?

He didn't think so. On the other hand, having been born rich and royal, he'd never had to make more than a minimal effort to get a woman into his bed.

Of course, Jewel didn't know he was rich and royal, and he was happy to keep it that way for now. If she knew his true identity, she'd likely use it as an excuse to fire him and he'd probably never see her again.

And he wasn't nearly ready to say goodbye to Jewel Callahan. She was the most intriguing and frustrating woman he'd ever met, and every step she took in retreat only made him more determined to advance.

Her comments about his youth suggested that she was bothered by the age difference between them. Though he didn't know exactly what that difference was, he wasn't worried about it. He'd had other lovers who were older—one or two who were definitely older than Jewel—and age had never been an issue for him.

Nor was the fact that she was his boss. Not that he'd ever had an affair with an employer, and in fact, royal duties aside, he'd never really had a job before. But he sensed that the employer-employee relationship would present another problem for Jewel, another explanation for her resistance.

Disregarding both the age and employment issues, he'd forced himself to consider the possibility that she simply might not be interested. And he'd discarded that thought the minute he took her in his arms on the dance floor.

There had been a definite spark between them, and a wary awareness in the depths of those stormy eyes.

She might pretend she was uninterested, but he knew differently.

Just as he knew that if he pushed her for too much too soon, she'd push him away.

He'd never been a patient man—he'd never had to be. But he knew that seducing Jewel was going to require both patience and perseverance—and that the end result would be worth the effort.

With that thought in mind, he stripped off his clothes and climbed into bed. The sheets were crisp and cool against his heated skin, but he knew nothing and no one but Jewel would douse the fire in his blood.

Chapter Five

It was the end of a long day at the end of a long week, and it seemed to Jewel that she hadn't had much time to spend at Haven recently. Probably because she'd been so busy trying to court new clients for CTC in case Gabe Anderson followed through on his threat to withdraw his horses from the stables. Which was why, at the end of yet another eighteen-hour day, she found herself heading to the stables instead of her bed. Tired and cranky as she felt, she didn't want to short-change Haven's residents.

She moved through the barn, checking water buckets and hay nets along the way, noting the cleanliness of the stalls, the gleaming coats of the horses. When she reached Wizard's stall, she noticed the horse was swaying from side to side, a sure sign that he was bored and needed exercise. Despite her fatigue, she decided to take him out onto the track.

But she paused at Cayenne's stall first, spoke briefly to the skittish stallion and coaxed him to take an apple. The stallion snorted his protest when she moved on, and pawed impatiently at the ground.

She felt herself waver. Cayenne was a big animal—almost seventeen hands—and spirited, and all of her student helpers were terrified of him. He was also one of her favorites.

His pedigree wasn't anything spectacular, but that didn't matter to anyone who had seen him run. He was purchased for a paltry sum at the Keeneland September Yearling Sale and won a substantial amount of money for his owner in the next ten months.

Then there was an accident at the stables—the horse got spooked and kicked out at the owner's six-year-old daughter. The child suffered broken ribs and bruised kidneys; her father beat the colt within an inch of his life then abandoned him in a distant pasture. He stayed there, injured, isolated, neglected, for more than six months before anyone contacted Haven.

He'd been with Jewel for almost a year now and both she and Crystal had gradually managed to earn the stallion's trust. He was still wary of everyone else, however, and men in particular.

There had been some interest in him when he first came to Haven, potential buyers who remembered his early performances as a two-year-old, who understood that the horse shouldn't be held responsible for an accident that occurred because a child was left unsupervised in the barn. But the interest waned when they realized the skittish animal wouldn't let visitors come near enough to examine him never mind put a saddle on his back.

He'd made significant progress in the past twelve months,

but Jewel worried that she might have already missed out on any opportunities to find him a good home.

"Tomorrow," she promised, and gave him a last pat before gathering her tack and grooming kit, then heading back to Wizard's stall.

She opened the door and the old gelding came to her, butting his head gently against her shoulder in greeting. Smiling, she took another apple from her pocket and offered it to him. He took it happily—and more mannerly than Cayenne had done.

She led him out of the stall and gave him a quick grooming, pleased to see that the high school kids who had been helping out had done a good job of that already. She positioned the blanket then slid the saddle onto his back. Recognizing the feel and weight of it, the gelding trembled with barely suppressed excitement.

"You remember, don't you?" she said softly. "The crowds, the excitement of the race, the thrill of victory."

The horse snorted again and tossed his head in agreement.

"And some people say that animals can't talk," a familiar male voice noted from over Jewel's shoulder.

She finished buckling the girth before she turned, but her heart was already pounding with recognition—and anticipation. "I'm not so sure about talking, but he definitely knows how to communicate."

Mac stepped closer, so that he was no longer hidden in the shadows, and her heart pounded even harder.

She eased the bridle over the horse's head, grateful to focus her attention on the task rather than the man who had dominated her thoughts far too often lately. Wizard took the bit eagerly.

"What's his story?" Mac asked, watching as she buckled the nose and chin straps.

"He has good bloodlines, but even as a yearling, he was out-of-control—too spirited to train never mind race. So his owners decided to geld him, thinking that would settle him down. It did, and he spent several years on the circuit. He finished in the money more often than not in his career, but never big money. When he started to slow down, his owners didn't know what to do with him. They couldn't retire him to stud, obviously, so they were going to put him down."

She saw the muscle in his jaw tighten, and knew he was as infuriated as she had been at the thought of a horse being euthanized simply because it was no longer winning races.

But when he spoke, it was only to ask, "How did you find him?"

"A friend of a friend."

"And what are your plans for him?"

"The same as all of the other horses that come here—to try to find him a new home. But right now—" she rubbed her hand over Wizard's cheek "—we're going to ride."

"Does he prefer to ride alone?"

She shrugged. "He just likes to ride, and he doesn't get nearly enough opportunities these days."

"Why don't you let me saddle up one of the other horses and go out with you?"

"You don't have anything better to do?"

"Not right now."

"Okay, then." She considered for a moment. "Peaches is overdue for a run."

Mac nodded, apparently unfazed at being asked to ride a horse named after a fruit. "Give me ten minutes to saddle her up."

* * *

Jewel mounted the gray and trotted him around while they waited for Mac.

She wasn't surprised when he took less than the ten minutes he'd asked for. She still had questions about him, but she no longer doubted his aptitude or abilities where the horses were concerned. And if she wished she knew a little bit more about the man, she reminded herself that nothing was as important as his doing the job he was hired to do.

She let Wizard begin to canter, and Peaches pulled up alongside, keeping the easy pace. Mac didn't seem to have any trouble handling the spirited mare. It was as if he instinctively knew when to exercise control and when to let the horse take the lead so that it didn't turn into a battle of wills—a battle that no man could win against a thousand-pound horse, though there were many who were foolish enough to try.

Mac didn't strike her as the foolish sort.

Though she wondered about the wisdom of her own actions in agreeing to a moonlight ride with a man who stirred feelings inside of her that hadn't been stirred in a very long time.

"This is quite the place you've got here," he said, as they guided their respective mounts toward the dirt oval.

She looked around, at the grounds and buildings that were the landscape of not just her business but her life, and felt a sense of contentment and satisfaction. She still marveled sometimes at the fact that everything she saw—as far as her eyes could see—was hers.

"There are times I still can't believe it was a twist of fate that made it mine," she said softly.

"Fate?"

"Long story."

"And one you don't particularly want to talk about," he guessed.

"It's not really a big secret, and if you hang around long enough, someone is bound to comment on the fact that I'm only running CTC because my father was killed on the way to his lawyer's office to change his will."

"He was going to write you out of it?"

She shook her head. "Nothing that drastic. I might not have been the son he wanted, but I was still his oldest child and he wanted the business to stay in the family. But he also wanted all the decisions to be made by his hand-picked management team, including his lawyer, Russ, and Brian Murray."

"That would be the same Brian Murray who owns the place down the street—the one your father wanted you to marry?"

She turned to glance at him over her shoulder. "Is there anything my sister hasn't told you?"

"She didn't give me any details," he told her. "So why don't you tell me about this marriage your father tried to arrange?"

"He wanted me to marry Brian in order to merge the two businesses. When I told him it wasn't going to happen, he decided that I was incapable of making decisions for myself. If I wouldn't accept Brian as my husband, I'd have to take him as my boss."

"And what were Brian's thoughts on all of this?"

"He wanted the merger. He made enough money betting on horses that he decided to try his hand at owning a few, then breeding one or two. After a dozen years in the business, he realized it was going to take a lot longer than that to build the kind of reputation Callahan has."

"Unless he married a Callahan," Mac guessed.

She nodded.

"And yet you managed to resist such a temptingly romantic offer," he said dryly.

She smiled at that. "Hard to believe, but somehow I did."

"Still, it must have been hard to lose your father when you had those kind of issues unresolved between you."

"The only thing that would be different if he hadn't died that day is CTC wouldn't be mine."

"What about your sister? Where does she fit into this?"

"I bought out her share of this business, then Crystal helped me found Haven."

"And this—" he gestured expansively "—is this what you've always wanted?"

"No." She grinned. "I used to want to be a champion barrel racer."

"What changed your mind?"

"Six years on the rodeo circuit. It seemed there was always one more town, one more season, and I realized I didn't want to spend my life on the road, moving from one hotel room to the next. I wanted a home—and a family."

"And so you gave up barrel racing and came home to train thoroughbreds."

"I came home," she agreed. "Though CTC requires that I spend more time with paperwork than the horses."

"I can't imagine that," he said, "considering how much time you spend in the stables and at the track."

She smiled. "It's my job to know what's happening with every one of the horses."

"You mentioned that you came back here because you were tired of life on the road—that you wanted a home and a family."

She nodded.

"So why aren't you married?" he asked.

Her eyes clouded. "Because life doesn't always work out the way we hope it will."

"Sometimes that's not a bad thing."

"What are *your* plans?" she asked.

He shrugged. "Nothing's carved in stone right now."

"You said you had a business degree," she recalled. "Why aren't you looking for a job in business?"

He felt a twinge of guilt. It wasn't so much that he'd lied to her as that he hadn't been entirely honest. He'd done more than study business—he'd earned a master's in business administration before continuing his education at law school. But he knew that if he'd admitted all of that, Jewel would have a lot more questions about why he was working as a stable hand at CTC, questions that he wasn't sure he was ready to answer.

"I'm just taking some time to do what I want to do first," he said, speaking the truth if not all of it. "I missed the horses, the physical labor of working in the stables, while I was at school. I'm looking at this as an opportunity to recharge before I spend the rest of my life at a real job."

"You don't think of what you're doing here as a real job?" she challenged.

He grinned and shook his head. "This has always been my passion—so much that I almost feel guilty earning money for doing it."

She laughed. "I'm not sure that's something you should admit to the woman signing your paychecks."

"That makes things a little bit awkward, doesn't it?"

"How so?"

He held her captive with nothing more than his gaze. "Because I really want to kiss you."

She knew what it meant when a man looked at a woman

the way he was looking at her, and she knew that they were treading on dangerous ground. "That would make things more than awkward."

"I know." He smiled. "Doesn't make me stop wanting you, though."

"I can't get involved with you, Mac."

"Why not?"

"For starters, you work for me."

"Okay, I quit."

She laughed, though the intensity with which he was staring at her made her suspect that he wasn't entirely joking. As they came upon the track, she could feel Wizard quivering with excitement and was grateful for the opportunity to end their conversation. "Are we going to talk or ride?"

"If those are my only two options—"

Jewel didn't wait to hear his response. She loosened the reins and Wizard, sensing his freedom, took off like a shot.

She heard Mac shout—a combination of surprise and protest—and then he gave chase.

Wizard got off to a good start and had an impressive lead over the mare coming up to the first marker. His eagerness and experience allowed him to hold on to the lead over the younger horse for a while longer, but they were neck-in-neck coming into the backstretch. Then, not surprisingly, Mac and Peaches edged ahead. But Wizard didn't let up. He fought back valiantly, racing with his heart as much as his legs, and approached the final post neck-in-neck with the other horse. When they crossed the imaginary wire, he'd actually stretched his nose out to take the mock race by a nod.

Jewel slid off of Wizard's back and wrapped her arms around his damp neck. "You were incredible," she told him.

"And you," Mac said from behind her, "are a speed junkie."

She turned around, grinning. "I have to admit, I love the feel of the wind in my face."

"You must have been a force on the rodeo circuit."

"Three time national champion," she told him.

He took a step closer. "But not everything in life should be a race to the finish line."

"You're just saying that because you lost."

"It was a tie."

"You lost."

"You cheated."

She lifted a brow. "How do you figure?"

"You started first."

"Just because you were slow out of the gate—"

The rest of the words lodged in her throat when his arm snaked around her waist. "No one's ever accused me of being slow out of the gate."

"Well—" she gave herself a moment to acknowledge the delicious little sparks that zinged through her system "—you were this time."

"Maybe I was," he acknowledged, drawing her closer. "Or maybe I chose finesse over speed."

"You still lost."

He smiled. "I don't think so."

Then he kissed her.

And he definitely chose finesse over speed this time.

His lips brushed over hers—once, twice, testing, teasing—then settled.

And Jewel realized he was right. In this, at least, she didn't want to hurry at all.

He kissed her softly, slowly and very thoroughly.

His tongue glided over her lips and she felt the sizzle right down to her toes, a jolt of electricity that melted the last of her resistance along with everything else inside of her.

Her hands were on his shoulders now, her fingers digging into the taut muscles, trying to hold herself steady in a world that was suddenly spinning out of control.

His hands slid up her back and down again, and she trembled against him. It had been a long time since she'd had a man's hands on her—so long, in fact, she'd almost forgotten how it felt to be touched, wanted, cherished. And she almost didn't want him to stop.

His hands skimmed upward again, over her ribs, the sides of her breasts, and she sighed.

She definitely didn't want him to stop.

But somewhere in the back of her mind, she knew that there were too many obstacles to a personal relationship between them.

He'd graduated from Harvard—she'd chosen the rodeo circuit over college. She'd eventually got her trainer's certificate and later picked up some night courses at the local college to help with the running of her business, but nothing that compared to his Ivy League education.

How he happened to be working for her right now was nothing more than some kind of cosmic fluke, an inexplicable mystery that could change in a heartbeat.

Then there was the obvious age gap. It still boggled her mind that she should be so intensely attracted to a man who was closer to twenty than thirty when she could see forty in the distance. So as good-looking and smart and sexy as he was—and every one of her hormones was in full agreement with that assessment—she couldn't forget that he was young enough to be…a much younger brother.

And it was just a cruel twist of fate that he could kiss with such masterful skill that an ordinarily sane and rational woman would be tempted to forget all of the reasons that she shouldn't jump into bed with him.

She pulled away, and drew in a long, deep breath.

Mac didn't protest her withdrawal. In fact, he didn't say anything at all, but only stroked a hand down her back in a gesture that was somehow both soothing and arousing.

"I can't do this, Mac." Her lips were still tingling from the pressure of his, and her body was still quivering with longing. It would be so easy to lean into him again, to let him take her where they both wanted to go. Instead she took a step back. "I need you here, at CTC, and I can't afford to lose you if I let things get personal."

"I'm not going to push for more than you're ready to give," he promised her. "But you should know two things—I'm not going anywhere, and things are already personal."

Chapter Six

The man was driving her mad.

Five days after Mac had kissed her, Jewel had barely caught sight of the man around the stables. Oh, she knew he was there, knew he'd been doing his job as well as putting in extra hours at Haven. But he hadn't sought her out, and though thoughts of him had hovered at the back of her mind, she sure as heck wasn't going to go looking for him.

The cocky self-confidence that fit him as nicely as his faded Levi's suggested that he was well aware of the effect he had on women, and she refused to swoon like the masses. She refused to admit that her heart did beat a little bit faster and her blood pulsed a little bit hotter whenever he was near.

It had been so long since she'd been attracted to any man that she couldn't help but wonder what it was about this one that kicked her hormones into overdrive. She frowned over that thought for a minute before considering that maybe it wasn't this man at all. Maybe it was simply…proximity.

After almost three years of self-imposed celibacy it was a logical explanation. And even before that, her affair with Allan hadn't been much more than a fling, and a somewhat disappointing one.

She'd hooked up with him a few months after Crystal had gotten married, after waking up one morning and realizing she was thirty-one years old and tired of going to bed alone every night. In retrospect, she realized she hadn't been attracted to him so much as she'd been attracted to the idea of being with someone. The relationship had lasted all of three months and she'd been more relieved than disappointed when they'd both finally agreed it wasn't working.

There had been no one since then. She'd wanted no one since then—until Mac Delgado had walked into the Halfway Café.

The knock on the door jolted her from her reverie.

The sight of the man himself standing in her doorway jolted all of her hormones to attention.

"Are you busy?" Mac asked.

"I'm always busy," she said, as much to remind herself as him that she didn't have time for anything other than business, and certainly no time to be distracted by the feelings he stirred in her.

"Too busy to take a drive into town to grab some dinner?"

She glanced at her watch, surprised to see that it was dinnertime already. And as Bonnie had gone to Michigan to visit her sister for a couple of weeks, there would be no dinner waiting for her when she finally headed up to the house.

But driving into town with Mac? Sitting at a table and sharing a meal with him? She wasn't sure that was a good idea. And, after five days of silence, she wasn't going to jump just because he'd asked her to.

"I'm not really hungry," she said, then felt her cheeks heat when her stomach chose that exact moment to growl in contradiction of her statement.

Mac grinned, and the flutters in her tummy were suddenly stronger than her appetite. "You sure?"

She sighed, because it was just dinner. And the fact that she hadn't seen or heard from him in the past few days was a pretty good indication that she'd misinterpreted his feelings for her, overreacted to a casual look, an innocent touch, and a single mind-numbing kiss.

"Okay," she admitted, "I am hungry, but I've got some things I have to finish up here and—"

"I'll wait."

"As much as I appreciate the invitation," she continued, "I'm going to be a while so you should just go ahead."

He shrugged. "Your call."

She forced a smile, refusing to acknowledge the twinge of disappointment she felt that he'd relented so easily. "Enjoy your dinner."

Nearly an hour passed before Jewel shut down her computer and returned to the house. She was comparing the merits of leftover week-old lasagna and microwave popcorn when there was a knock at the door.

"You said you wouldn't go out for dinner with me," Mac said. "You didn't say you wouldn't share a pizza with me if I brought it to you."

She opened the door wider, too tempted by the flat cardboard box in his hand to turn him away.

He grinned as he stepped into the house, while she worried that she'd made the wrong choice in refusing to go out with him earlier. Sharing a meal in a public restaurant seemed much less risky than inviting him into her house, where they would be alone together. And that thought was niggling at her mind even before he passed her the bottle of wine he carried in his other hand.

She frowned at the familiar label as she asked, "What's on the pizza?"

"Pepperoni, sausage, hot peppers and olives."

"Did you happen to run into my sister in town?"

"As a matter of fact, she and her husband were in line at the movie theater."

Which was, coincidentally, right next door to the pizza parlor.

"Nice guy—Simon," he said. "Though he certainly isn't the type of guy I would have expected your sister to marry."

It was the reaction most people had when they met Crystal—who still looked like the perky cheerleader she'd been in high school, and Simon—a stereotypical nerd with thick glasses and thinning air. The technologically challenged dessert chef and the diabetic computer geek, as Crystal referred to them. And yet, there was no denying that they were madly in love and truly committed to one another.

While Jewel got the plates and napkins, Mac opened and closed drawers until he found the corkscrew.

"By the way," he continued, "they're having a dinner party in a couple of weeks. Simon said you already know some of the other guests, so he's putting you on the invite list, and Crystal suggested that you should bring me as your date."

"My sister has a habit of sticking her nose into things that are none of her business," Jewel told him.

"She thought the merlot might persuade you to at least

consider it." He deftly uncorked the bottle and poured it into the two glasses she'd set on the counter.

She smiled at that. "It would take more than a bottle of wine—even if it is my favorite—to make me abandon all common sense and go out with a man I barely know, who is at least ten years younger than me, and an employee."

"I'm hardly a stranger, I'm only eight years younger than you, and as much as I'm enjoying this job, I'd give it up in a heartbeat if that's all it would take to get you to change your mind about going out with me."

As flattered as she was by the latter part of his statement, it was the middle that caused her to frown. "How do you know how old I am?" Then she shook her head. "Obviously from the same source that told you what toppings I like on my pizza."

"I was surprised," he admitted. "I wouldn't have guessed that you were a day over thirty."

"And I wouldn't have guessed that you were a day over twenty-two."

He shrugged. "So we were both wrong."

"And eight years is pretty close to ten."

He just smiled and handed her a plate with two slices of pizza on it. "Hungry?"

"Starving." She took the plate and pulled back a chair.

He took a seat on the other side of the table and loaded up his own plate.

"What movie were they going to see?" Jewel asked.

"The new Sandra Bullock film. Simon said it was a chick-flick, but he said it with such a dorky smile on his face, it was obvious he didn't mind."

"Or he was hoping to get lucky after the movie," she said dryly.

"And people say that I'm cynical," he noted, picking up his wineglass.

She slid into the chair across from him. "What else do they say about you?"

"That I'm attentive, considerate, charming—"

"Modest?"

He grinned and shook his head. "No one's ever accused me of that."

"Hard to believe."

They polished off the whole pizza, and while they ate, they talked about everything but nothing of importance. And as they talked, Marcus noticed that Jewel finally started to relax, her smile started to come more easily and her words were less censored.

"When I first saw you at the café with Crystal, I wouldn't have guessed that you were sisters."

"We're half sisters," she admitted.

"Same mother or father?"

"Father." She picked up her glass, took a long sip of wine before continuing. "My mom walked out before my third birthday. Jack hooked up with Alice—Crystal's mom—a few years later. Then she walked out, too, a few years after that, but she had the sense to take Crystal with her."

"And left you," he guessed.

She shrugged. "She was willing to take me, too, and told Jack she wanted us to stay together. Jack wouldn't hear of it—not that he wanted me around, but he didn't want anyone else to take what was his. And since she wasn't my mother, she had no legal claim to custody.

"She kept in touch for a few years—bringing Crystal back

for regular visits—more for me than Jack. Then she remarried and moved to Washington.

"When Crystal was twelve, Alice and her husband were killed in a car accident. She was sent back here to live with Jack, but I was already gone."

And she felt guilty about that, he could tell. She'd spent her whole life being neglected by the man who'd fathered her and wanted only to save her little sister from the same fate.

"That's when you ran off to be a rodeo star?" he asked lightly.

"Something like that."

They ate in companionable silence for a few minutes, then Marcus heard himself say, "My mom died when I was seven."

She looked up, surprise and compassion evident in her beautiful blue-gray eyes. "That must have been hard."

He wasn't sure why he told her that—it certainly wasn't a usual topic of conversation. In fact, he couldn't remember sharing such personal details with a woman. But when she reached across the table to touch her hand to his arm, he realized the explanation might be as simple as that he'd never met another woman who would understand as he'd known Jewel would.

"How did she die?" she asked gently.

"A brain aneurysm." And he'd taken so much for granted before she'd died. Being a prince had ensured there was almost nothing he couldn't have or do. Until all he'd wanted was his mother to wake up—and no one could make that happen for him.

"One minute she was there, and the next she was gone," Jewel murmured.

He knew the loss she'd experienced had been similar, that her scars probably ran as deep.

"Did your dad ever remarry?" she asked gently.

He shook his head. "My mom was the love of his life. After she died, he focused on his duties."

"Duties?"

He mentally cursed himself for the slip and quickly amended, "His job."

"And he raised you on his own?"

He managed to smile now, thinking of his father with genuine love and affection. "My father didn't have a clue about raising kids," he admitted. "But he did have a nanny."

"A nanny," she echoed and leaned back in her chair, removing her hand from his arm so that it felt almost cold after the warmth of her touch. "Which again makes me wonder—what the heck are you doing mucking out my barn?"

"Have you been dissatisfied with my work?"

"You know that's not what I mean."

"I like my job here, and I think I've proven that I'm good at it. Why does anything else matter?"

"Because you're a Harvard graduate working as a stable hand."

He refilled her glass. "You're making this more complicated than it needs to be."

"I doubt that." She traced the base of her glass with her fingertip, her brow furrowed. "You don't fit in here, Mac.

"I'm not talking about your work," she continued. "You obviously know horses, and I'm grateful that you signed on. But you're not the drifter you're pretending to be."

"That's exactly what I am," he told her.

She shook her head. "Drifting from place to place, from job to job, doesn't make a man like you a drifter."

He quirked a brow. "What does it make me?"

"I haven't quite figured it out," she admitted.

"Maybe I'm just a man who's trying to figure out his place in the world."

"Maybe." But she didn't sound convinced. "If I had to guess, though, I'd say you were running from something."

He smiled, as if he was amused by her assessment when, in fact, he was a little unnerved by the accuracy of it. "A fugitive from the law?"

She sipped her wine. "Nothing so dramatic. More likely family expectations and responsibilities." She looked at him over the rim of her glass, considering. "I'd bet you have family connections to the Vanderbilts or Rockefellers or Kennedys. And you probably have some blueblood fiancée back in Boston who you convinced you needed to take some time for yourself before you settled down."

"There's no fiancée. Not in Boston or anywhere else." He laid his hand over hers, and this touch had nothing to do with offering comfort or compassion, and they both knew it. Her breath caught before her eyes lifted slowly to meet his. His thumb brushed over her wrist, felt her pulse race. "I wouldn't be here with you if there was."

"And this is why having dinner together was a bad idea," she said softly.

"I think it was a good idea," he said. "We finally had a chance to talk about something more personal than horses and manure, and now you can't say I'm a stranger anymore."

She pulled her hand away. "You're still ten years younger than me."

"Eight," he corrected again.

"And somehow, despite the age factor weighing on my side, I get the impression I'd be totally out of my league with you."

"Personal relationships aren't team sports."

"No," she agreed. "But they often do involve a lot of game-playing, and I don't have the interest or inclination."

He felt his lips curve. "Are you going to tell me that you haven't thought about it?"

"I've occasionally considered a foolish course of action, but recognizing it as such usually prevents the mistake from being made."

"Usually?"

She swallowed. "I can't afford to make any mistakes at this point in my life."

Everything she was feeling was in her eyes—attraction, confusion, desire and uncertainty. It was the uncertainty that held him back. As much as he wanted her, he needed to know that she wanted the same thing.

Until then, he would force himself to be patient.

Tearing his gaze from hers, he glanced at the clock on the stove. "I didn't realize it was getting to be so late."

"Neither did I," she admitted.

He pushed away from the table. "I should go."

She nodded and got up to walk him to the door.

"Mac?" She touched a hand to his arm, forcing him to turn back, to look into those gorgeous blue-gray eyes that were shining a little brighter than usual because of the wine, cheeks that were flushed, lips that were slightly parted.

He had to remind himself of his vow to be patient. "Yes?"

The tip of her tongue swept along the curve of her bottom lip. "Thanks for the pizza. And the company."

He curled his fingers into his palms to resist the urge to reach for her. "You're welcome."

Chapter Seven

Jewel wasn't surprised when Crystal popped by her office late the next morning. An impromptu visit from her sister was a rare occurrence, but Jewel didn't need two guesses to ascertain the reason for this one.

"Aren't you supposed to be at work?" she asked.

"The morning rush is over," Crystal said. "And the blueberry muffins just came out of the oven, so I thought I'd take a break to see how you were doing."

Jewel opened the paper sack her sister set on her desk and hummed her approval at the mouthwatering scent that wafted out.

"Apparently I'm hungry," she said, reaching into the bag.

"Probably because you haven't eaten anything since the pizza you had for dinner last night."

"Thanks for that, by the way."

Crystal looked wary. "You're not going to chastise me for matchmaking?"

"I didn't realize you were," she fibbed as she broke the top off of a muffin. "I thought you were just ensuring that I had something to eat."

Her sister huffed out a breath. "Are you honestly telling me that you shared pizza and a bottle of wine with Mac last night and *nothing* happened?"

"We talked."

"He didn't even kiss you?"

She considered her answer while she chewed, and decided evasion was the safest response. "Why all the interest in my personal life all of a sudden?"

"Because you seem to have a personal life all of a sudden."

Jewel took another bite of muffin. "Does that mean you'll be wanting all the details of how we did it on the kitchen table after we finished the pizza?"

"You didn't do it on the kitchen table or anywhere else," Crystal stated confidently.

"How do you know?"

"Because if you had, you'd be looking a lot more relaxed than you do right now."

"Maybe he just isn't very good."

Crystal smirked. "Do you really expect me to believe that?"

"I expect you to know me better than to think I would fall into bed with a man I've barely known three weeks."

"I fell in love with Simon after only three days," Crystal told her.

"Thanks for the muffins," Jewel said, trying to nudge her sister along. "But I have a dozen things—"

"I didn't only come here to bring you muffins," Crystal interjected. "Or to dig for information about Mac."

Jewel looked at her sister, only now noticing the extra sparkle in her eyes, the natural flush of color in her cheeks. And that suddenly, she knew what Crystal had come to tell her.

Her baby sister was going to have a baby.

Jewel was stunned, thrilled—and a tiny bit envious. But it was only after she'd finally said goodbye and Crystal had gone that the tears came.

There were tears of joy for her sister, who had been trying for so long to start a family with her husband. And tears for herself, because while Crystal's dreams were finally starting to come true, her own were still so far out of reach.

It was the click of the latch as the door closed that warned Jewel she was no longer alone even before Mac knelt down beside her. "What's wrong?"

She brushed the moisture from her cheeks, as embarrassed to have been caught indulging in such an emotional display as she was ashamed of the selfish nature of her tears. "Nothing."

"It doesn't look like nothing."

"I just found out my sister is going to have a baby," she told him.

"Crystal?"

She managed a smile. "She's the only sister I have—the only family I have."

He pulled a tissue from the box on her desk and gently wiped her eyes. "When's she due?"

"January."

Mac smiled. "My brother's wife is expecting their first child in a couple of months."

"I didn't know you had a brother."

"Two of them, in fact." His eyes clouded for a moment before he said, "There used to be four of us, before my eldest brother and his wife died in a boating accident."

"I'm sorry."

He shook his head. "I'm sorry," he said. "We were talking about your happy news. I didn't mean to put a damper on the conversation."

She reached out and touched a hand to his arm. "How long ago did your brother and his wife die?"

His gaze dropped to her hand, as if he was surprised by her touch. And though she was suddenly conscious of the taut muscle in his forearm and the heat of his skin, she didn't pull away.

"Two and a half years," he said.

He was still grieving, she could hear it in his voice. She knew as well as anyone that time didn't really heal all wounds, it just made the pain a little more bearable.

"Did they have any kids?" she asked.

He nodded. "Three."

He heart ached for those children, and she found herself thinking about the loss of her own mother—a woman whose presence was taken from her daughter's life not by the fickle hand of fate but through her own conscious choice, and wondered why it somehow seemed even harder to accept that the woman who'd given birth to her hadn't loved her enough to stay.

She pushed the thought aside, refused to let the bitter memories cast a pall over the moment.

"So you have nieces? Nephews?"

"One niece, two nephews, so far."

"Do you see them often?"

"Not as much as I'd like in the past few years," he said.

"They live far away?"

His lips quirked just a little. "Yeah."

That was all he said, and though it was an answer to her question, she was somehow more aware of what he didn't say, the information he held back, evidence of yet another secret between them.

She wanted to press him for more, to learn the answers to all the questions she had about him. He'd given her little pieces of himself, yet she sensed there was still so much that she didn't know.

"They're in Europe," he finally said. "My family lives on an island in the Mediterranean."

"Oh." She was surprised by the revelation and glad that he'd finally volunteered some information. "You don't sound European," she said inanely. "Except—" she broke off, her cheeks flushing.

"Except?" he prompted.

Her cheeks burned hotter. "When you're flirting with me," she admitted. "Then your voice deepens and picks up just the slightest hint of an accent."

He touched a hand to her cheek, the lazy stroke of his thumb over her skin causing shivers to dance down her spine. "Does it?"

And just those two words, and the light touch, had everything inside her quivering.

She forced herself to take a mental step back, to remind herself—to remind both of them—how ill-suited they were.

"I want a baby."

She hadn't intended to blurt out that thought, but when his face went pale, she couldn't help but laugh.

"I didn't mean right now, and I certainly didn't mean with you."

He frowned at that. "Why 'certainly' not with me?"

She shook her head. "You've made it clear that you have no interest in a serious relationship, never mind marriage or children, yet you're somehow offended by the statement that I don't want to have a child with you."

"Well, it's not flattering for a man to be told he's not good father material."

"You'd probably make a great father," she said. "When you stopped being such a child."

"Ouch."

She laughed again. "I couldn't resist—your instinctive panicked reaction was just so typical."

"Typical?" He sounded more offended by that than being referred to as a child.

Jewel waved the question aside. "I assume there was a reason you're here—other than to wipe my tears?"

"Yeah." He stroked a finger over the curve of her bottom lip. "That was just a bonus."

"The reason?" she prompted.

"Cayenne."

She jumped to her feet.

"Nothing's wrong," he hastened to assure her. "I just wanted to let you know that Harold Emerson was looking at him today—and hinting that he might be interested in adding him to his stable."

"He wants to buy Cayenne?"

"Maybe."

She understood his caution—but any interest in the way-ward stallion at this point was far more than she'd expected.

Impulsively she threw her arms around his neck and gave him a smacking kiss on the lips. "This is almost as good as Crystal's news."

"And that was even better," he said, tightening his arm around her when she started to draw back and kissing her again.

What it was, she immediately realized, was a mistake. Because the minute his mouth took possession of hers, she wanted more.

In the time that had passed since their first kiss, she'd managed to reassure herself that she'd been smart to put on the brakes, that she couldn't have an affair with him. She'd even managed to convince herself that the kiss wasn't as spectacular as she'd remembered. It was just that it had been so very long since she'd been kissed that she'd exaggerated both his skill and her response.

This kiss blasted that theory to smithereens.

And when his tongue touched hers, her mind went completely blank. There was no thought or reason. There was nothing but Mac and an acceptance of the passion that had been simmering between them since the first—a passion that was everything she hadn't even known she'd wanted.

But now, there was no denying how very much she wanted. She wrapped her arms around him, pressed her body closer to his to absorb his warmth, his touch, his taste.

His hands slid up her back, her breasts brushed his chest and sparks of electric heat zinged through her system.

Oh, yeah, he knew how to kiss.

His mouth moved over hers with a skillful mastery that made everything inside her tremble and yearn. His hands tangled in her hair, tipping her head back. His tongue dove deeper between her parted lips, tasting, tempting.

It seemed as if he would kiss her forever, and she knew that even if he did, forever wouldn't be long enough. So she let herself savor the moment, steeped herself in his flavor and gloried in the press of his hot, hard body against hers.

"Usted me está conduciendo insano." He murmured the words against her lips.

"I have no idea what you just said," she told him.

"I said you are driving me crazy," he admitted. "When are you going to stop torturing me?"

"Believe it or not," she said, "I'm not trying to torture you."

He nibbled on her lip as his hand found her breast, his thumb circled the nipple, testing, teasing. "Just a coincidence then?"

Her only response was a moan, deep in her throat, when his thumb brushed over the turgid peak.

He said something else, speaking softly again in Spanish. She didn't understand the words—she didn't need to. The tone was pure seduction, and she was helplessly entranced.

She didn't realize he'd unfastened her shirt until his lips moved down her throat, then lower to nuzzle between her breasts. His cheek was rough against her sensitive skin, his breath was warm, and the little flicks of his tongue were deliciously erotic.

He freed one breast from the lacy constraint of her bra, then his mouth was on her, hot and hungry. She gasped as fiery spears of pleasure arrowed to her core. Her fingers dug into his shoulders, holding on while the earth seemed to tilt on its axis.

She was tempted—oh, so tempted—to follow where he was leading, to let her world spin out of control. But she was afraid—of the desire she tasted in his kiss, of the needs churning inside herself, of the enormity of feelings she hadn't known before. And her fear was stronger than her desire.

She pulled out of his arms and drew in a long, shuddering breath as she refastened the buttons of her shirt.

Mac lifted a hand, as if to touch her, and she took another quick step back, out of reach. Her blood was still pulsing, her body aching, and she wasn't entirely sure she could be trusted not to jump his bones if he touched her again right now.

His hand dropped to his side.

"I'm not playing hard to get," she told him. "I'm just not looking for a relationship right now, or a quick fling, or anything else you might be thinking of."

"I was thinking it wouldn't be quick," he said, in a tone that had her blood pulsing again.

She swallowed, hard. "Mac."

"You know what I want, Jewel. The next step is yours."

And then he was gone, and she was left alone and wanting.

Marcus was up earlier than usual on race day, and though there was a lot of work that needed to be done, he stole a private moment to make his weekly telephone call home. It was Lara who answered the prince regent's private line, and the pleasure and warmth in her voice made him feel just a little bit homesick.

"We weren't expecting you to call until tomorrow," she said. "Rowan's tied up in meetings all day today."

"I'm going to be out most of the day tomorrow," he told her. "And I'd rather talk to you anyway, so I'm glad I caught you."

"It's easy to catch me these days," she admitted. "It's hard to move fast when you waddle."

He chuckled. "Rowan e-mailed me some photos—you're not that huge yet."

"Now that I'm in my seventh month, I seem to be getting

bigger every day." Then, in an obvious change of subject, "Tell me what you've been up to."

"Working."

"And loving every minute of it, I can tell."

"It's been a good experience," he agreed.

"You've been there several weeks already," she noted. "And you're not getting bored yet?"

"No. In fact, I can't remember when I've had more fun."

"Mucking out stalls?" she asked dubiously.

"I've met someone," he admitted. He wouldn't have confided the fact in his brother, but he'd always found it easy to talk to Lara.

"A female someone, I'm guessing."

Marcus grinned. "Yeah."

"Details," Lara demanded.

"She's beautiful and smart and sexy."

"Does she have a name?"

"Her name is Jewel."

"You sound smitten, Marcus." And she sounded genuinely pleased by that fact.

"I think I am," he admitted.

"When am I going to get to meet her?"

"Well, that might be a bit of a problem."

Lara groaned. "She doesn't know who you are, does she?"

"I'm going to tell her."

"When?"

"When I'm sure that it won't make a difference."

His sister-in-law sighed.

"How are things there?" he asked, in a deliberate attempt to deflect the inevitable lecture.

"We're gearing up for the Independence Celebrations."

"I hope you're not overdoing it."

He could picture Lara rolling her eyes as she responded to his comment. "Rowan is hardly letting me do anything, and when he's not here to keep an eye on me, he's got someone else hovering."

Marcus smiled. "How are the kids?"

"They're doing great," she assured him. "But they miss you and keep asking when Uncle Marcus is coming home."

"I miss all of you, too," he said. "And you can tell them I'll be home for the celebrations, if not sooner."

"Will you be coming alone?"

Marcus smiled at his sister-in-law's subtle prodding. "I'll let you know."

Jewel had been at the track since before dawn, when the grandstands had stood silent and empty and the infield was covered with mist. Now it was nearing post time, and the stands were quickly filling up. There was an energy in the air—a buzz of excitement and anticipation.

She had a *Daily Racing Form* in her pocket and had placed her minimum bets. She'd never been much of a gambler and didn't pay any attention to odds or handicaps, but she believed in making a customary wager to demonstrate confidence and faith in her horses.

After Midnight was entered in the fourth race on the ticket, and though the horses for the third were just now being escorted onto the track, it was After Midnight that was on her mind. She needed him to race well today. Gabe Anderson had demanded it, and she'd known him long enough to know he was serious about his threat to take all of his horses elsewhere if he didn't get the results he wanted with After Midnight.

Over the past several years, there had been more than enough times when she'd wished she didn't have to deal with Anderson and his overinflated ego, but she'd put up with him simply because his defection could be a serious blow to CTC.

Caleb had assured her the colt was both ready and eager to race. Jewel knew she couldn't ask for more than that—though she wouldn't turn down a little luck.

"Nervous?"

She turned to find Mac beside her. "Do I look nervous?"

He studied her for a moment, and if she hadn't already been aware of the nerves in her belly, the intensity of his gaze would have started them stirring. "Maybe focused rather than nervous."

He took her hand, turned it over and pressed something against her palm.

She glanced at the pale blue stone, still warm from the heat of his hand, then at him. "What is it?"

"Aventurine," he told her. "For luck."

"You don't strike me as the type to carry lucky stones in his pocket."

He shrugged. "It was given to me by a friend—now I'm giving it to you."

She closed her fingers around the smooth, polished quartz. "Thanks."

The nerves in her belly jolted when the bell rang and the starting gates sprang open. Mac took up position beside her as the horses thundered onto the track, and though every nerve ending in her body was acutely aware of his nearness, she somehow found his presence comforting. Or maybe it was just the distraction from her other concerns that she appreciated.

She didn't even take notice of who won that race—it was the next one that held her attention.

She watched the post parade, noted the familiar royal and white colors that After Midnight and his jockey were wearing as they were escorted onto the track. Even from this distance, she could see the nervous excitement of the horse, the focused intensity of his rider, and she felt her own muscles knot in anticipation as After Midnight was loaded into the starting gate.

"Arianna's running later today, isn't she?" Mac asked.

"In the seventh."

"She looked good this morning," he said. "She knows why she's here, and she's ready for it."

Jewel nodded. "I'm not worried about Arianna."

"Then it's Gabe Anderson's entry that has you gripping the fence until your knuckles are white."

She pulled her hands back and tucked them into her pockets. "Don't you have work to do?"

There was no censure in her question, so he only lifted a shoulder in response. "There's always work to do, and so few opportunities to spend time with a beautiful woman."

Her brows lifted. "Flirting with your boss could be dangerous, Delgado."

"I keep hoping," he assured her.

"Mac—"

"I do have to get back to the shedrow," he interrupted. "But there was one more thing I need to do first."

And before she could even ask what it was, he touched his mouth to hers in a brief but potent kiss that had the knots in her stomach twisting for reasons that had nothing to do with the race about to take place.

"Was that for luck, too?" she asked when he drew away.

"No—" he grinned "—that was for me." Then he turned and walked off, whistling.

Chapter Eight

After Midnight came second in a field of nine. It was a more than respectable finish and the colt had run well, but Jewel knew Anderson would be ticked that his horse had given up the lead in the backstretch, coming under the wire almost two full lengths behind the winner.

She tucked her hands into her pockets as she went to rustle up a cup of coffee and found the stone Mac had given to her earlier. Russ had once said that she'd learned more than the business from her father—she'd learned to keep her emotions bottled up inside. Her cool demeanor and level-headedness had served her well in business, and she was a little unnerved that a man she'd known for such a short time had seen through the facade and recognized the feelings she'd managed to hide from everyone else. But she was also touched by the effort Mac had made to take her mind off of her worries, pleased by the thoughtfulness of his gesture.

She shook her head, wondering what was wrong with her that she was getting sentimental over a silly rock even as she reached into her pocket for it. It was just a stone—but it was a pretty stone. And while she didn't really believe it had helped After Midnight's performance, she didn't see any harm in holding on to it until after Arianna's race.

Mac didn't have any trouble picking Jewel out of the crowd, and while she watched the horses, he watched her.

When Arianna was led onto the track, her hands dipped into her pockets. He wondered if she was looking for the aventurine he'd given to her earlier for luck, or if she just wanted to make sure she couldn't twist her fingers together, as she sometimes did when she was anxious.

He saw her gaze zero in on the purple and gray silks her jockey wore and knew she probably didn't see anyone or anything else as the horses were loaded into the starting gate. Some of them entered more willingly than others, and it took a while before it was Arianna's turn. She'd drawn the tenth post position in a field of twelve, and though it was a little more outside than Jewel probably would have liked, he knew Arianna liked space to run. If she shot out to an early lead, as she liked to do, she could then move to the inside.

Caleb joined Jewel to watch the race, just as the horses sprang from the gate. Their hooves pounded like thunder in the dirt, and though it looked like a tight race, he was pleased to see that Arianna had already started to edge out in front. Steadily she moved forward, her legs stretching out, pulling her ahead of the pack, and seeming to increase her lead with every long stride. By the time she flew under the wire, she was more than five lengths ahead of her nearest competitor.

The next time he caught sight of Jewel, she was leaving the winner's circle with Arianna. She was waylaid several times on her way back to the shedrow by people she knew or other spectators just wanting to offer congratulations.

She smiled warmly at an older man who approached, nodding in response to something he said. Mac's attention shifted, along with Jewel's, to another man who was being introduced to her by the first, and his gaze narrowed.

No. It couldn't be...

The second man turned slightly, giving Mac a more direct view, and he felt his jaw clench instinctively as his suspicion was confirmed.

He was looking at none other than Prince Cameron Leandres.

Which led him to wonder—what the hell was his cousin doing in West Virginia? And, more importantly, did Cameron have any idea that Marcus was there? Because if he did, he could ruin everything.

Jewel let her groom lead Arianna back to the shedrow for a much-deserved rubdown and celebratory dinner while she turned her attention to Hugo DaCosta.

The older man was a former acquaintance of her father who had introduced himself to her earlier and expressed an interest in renewing a business relationship with CTC. Jewel had accepted his invitation to dinner in order to discuss the possibilities.

"I want you to meet a friend of mine," Hugo said to her now. "This is Prince Cameron Leandres of Tesoro del Mar."

"Nice to meet you." She offered her hand.

He caught her hand, but instead of shaking it, he brought it to his lips. "The pleasure is mine."

Though his charm seemed a little too practiced, he was good-looking. Not quite as tall as Mac, not quite as dark, and with eyes more hazel than brown—she broke off, appalled to realize she'd been comparing the two men, and forced her attention back to the one in front of her.

"Do you have an entry on the card?" she asked politely.

"No, I'm…observing today."

"And have you been impressed with what you've seen so far?"

He smiled as his eyes skimmed over her. "Very."

"Ms. Callahan owns and operates one of the finest training facilities in the state," DaCosta interjected.

"Some would say *the* finest," Jewel felt compelled to add.

DaCosta grinned. "And Cameron's family has one of the finest thoroughbred stables in his country."

"And I would argue that it is *the* finest," the prince told her. "Although Hugo has me thinking that I should invest in some quality racehorses in this country. Perhaps you could give me some advice."

There was something about the man, prince or not, that made her a little uneasy. But she was too savvy a business person to pass up such an opportunity. "And I'm guessing you would also need a local facility to board and train those horses."

"Of course," the prince agreed.

"Then you should come out to CTC and talk to Caleb Bryce," she suggested.

"I'd rather talk to you," he said.

"Excellent," DaCosta proclaimed. "You can discuss it over dinner."

* * *

Unfortunately there wasn't much of an opportunity to discuss business over dinner. The group that DaCosta had assembled numbered more than twenty, most of whom wanted only to talk about themselves and their personal successes. Even more unfortunately, Jewel found herself seated beside Prince Cameron, who demonstrated a fondness for personal contact. She managed to grit her teeth and tolerate it while it was just her shoulder or her arm that he was touching, but when his hand slipped beneath the tablecloth to her knee, her irritation threatened to overcome reason. Then his palm started to travel upward on her thigh.

Reaching beneath the table, she removed his hand from her thigh and held it up. "I believe this belongs to you," she told him.

He dropped his hand onto the back of her chair and leaned in to whisper in her ear. "I believe we're wasting our time here. Why don't we go back to my hotel room and continue our discussion in private?"

She pushed back her chair. "I really need to get back to the stables. If your interest in CTC is genuine, please feel free to stop by to visit the facilities."

The prince's gaze raked over her. "I'll do that."

Then he turned his attention, and his wandering hands, to the woman seated on his other side.

Jewel said a quick thank-you and goodbye to Hugo DaCosta before making her escape.

When she finally got home, she was tired but too wired to sleep. After a quick shower to scrub away the last remnants of the prince's groping touch, she went down to Haven and saddled up Daizy Mae. She hadn't realized how much she was looking forward to the possibility of seeing Mac until she felt her heart expand in her chest when she caught sight of him at the top of the hill.

She noted, with both surprise and amusement, that he'd chosen Medicine Man from the stable. The twenty-three-year-old stallion had little spark left in him and wasn't any kind of a challenge for an experienced rider like Mac. But like an elderly man trying to prove he was still useful, the old horse would trot or canter or gallop when prompted to do so.

"Interesting choice of mount," she noted.

He shrugged. "I figured they all needed a turn at some exercise."

"They do," she agreed, pleased that he'd recognized the fact. She was also pleased that he'd taken such an interest in Haven, even if she felt a slight twinge of guilt for the same reason. "I have to wonder—between your job at CTC and the extra hours you've been putting in at Haven—when do you find time to sleep?"

"Why don't you come up to my apartment after the horses are put to bed and find out?"

Coming so close on the heels of Cameron's crude invitation, she'd expected to be offended by his offer. But his words were without guile and his smile was easy, and she found herself smiling back.

"A tempting invitation," she assured him. "But I think I'll pass."

"An open invitation," he assured her, with another smile.

And though she realized she was probably missing out on what would undoubtedly be an incredible experience with Mac, she figured it was a fair trade for keeping her heart intact. She'd gotten to know him pretty well over the past few weeks and already started to care for him. If she let herself get any more personally involved, it could only lead to heartache when he left the farm. As he was planning to do when Grady returned.

Maybe she could convince him to stay a little longer—but for what purpose? He might be satisfied with his menial chores in the short-term, but they both knew he was destined for greater things. And she was destined to remain exactly where she was.

They rode together in silence for several minutes before Mac said, "I heard you had another confrontation with Anderson today."

"Good news travels fast."

"For what it's worth, he's an idiot."

She smiled. "He knew my dad for a lot of years and doesn't seem to accept that I do things differently than the infamous Jack Callahan did."

"Such as not run the business into the ground?"

Her head swiveled.

He shrugged. "People talk."

"I didn't think anyone knew," she said softly.

"The ones who do also know that you turned CTC around, and they respect and admire you for it."

"I'm...surprised," she admitted. "Spending so much time at the track lately, I've been hearing stories about my father. Listening to other people share their memories of him, contrasting their images with that of the man I knew."

"What do you remember differently?"

"Everything." She guided Daizy around a stand of trees toward the stream. "He did spend most of his weekends at the track, and not just checking on the horses we trained. He liked to gamble, and he liked to drink, and he liked women. And because he was good-looking and charismatic and didn't mind throwing his money around, the women liked him right back.

"Of course, none of them stuck around for very long. Not once they realized what a selfish sonofabitch he was, and more devoted to the gambling and drinking than he could ever be to any one woman."

"Even you?"

"Especially me. When he died—" She shook her head. "You wouldn't have believed the mess he left behind. It took more than two years after he was gone to straighten everything out, to put CTC firmly back in the black."

"And you tried to do it so that no one else knew," he mused. "Without asking anyone for help."

"In this business, reputation is more important than a lot of other things—I didn't want people speculating, clients worrying.

"I didn't build this place from the ground up, as Gabe Anderson likes to remind me my father did. But I built it back up, and only then, only when I knew the business was back on solid ground, did I start building the facilities for Haven."

"Did you ever consider doing something completely different?"

She shook her head as she dismounted to lead Daizy to the water to drink. Marcus followed her lead. "The horses have been my life for as long as I can remember. I never knew or wanted anything else. Except…"

"Except?" he prompted.

"There was a time when I thought about going to school to get a degree in animal husbandry and expand our breeding program."

"Why didn't you?"

She looked away. "It was made very clear to me that

breeding horses wasn't woman's work and that I was to choose a more appropriate occupation."

They were walking side by side in the moonlight, and he couldn't remember a staged scene that had ever felt more romantic. "But it's obvious that you love your horses."

"My father always said that a man who makes decisions based on emotion is a man who makes mistakes," she quoted.

"And he wouldn't consider an exception to that—even for his daughter?"

"Especially not for his daughter. It was bad enough that I had to be born female without compounding the mistake by acting like one."

The more he heard about Jack Callahan, the more Marcus was certain the man had been a sonofabitch. "I don't think I would have liked your father."

"I'm not sure many people did," she admitted. "But they admired and respected him."

"I admire you," he told her.

She managed a smile at that, and they walked a few more minutes in silence before she turned her head to study him in the moonlight.

"What about you?" she asked. "Are you doing what you want?"

He thought about his family, and about the responsibilities that were waiting for him back home. Responsibilities that he'd shirked for too long. Then he looked at Jewel, at the serious intensity in her stormy eyes, and there was no doubt about what he wanted.

"Right now—" he dipped his head toward her "—I'm doing exactly what I want."

And he settled his mouth over hers.

His hand moved up her back to cup her neck, his fingers sifting through her silky curls and tipping her head back to deepen the kiss. Her lips parted willingly for him, her tongue teased his. She was soft and warm and passionate, and he wanted her desperately.

"Usted es tan hermoso, tan perfecto." He whispered the words against her lips.

"I have no idea what you just said, but it sure sounded beautiful."

"Not as beautiful as you," he told her.

She drew away slightly. "You're trying to seduce me, aren't you?"

"No," he denied. "I told you the next move would have to be yours."

"And are you a man of your word?"

"Always." But he brushed his lips over hers once more before he drew away. "And because I am a man of my word, I should see you back to the stables before I forget that's true."

They rode back and tended to the horses in silence. It was only when they were walking out of the barn together that she spoke again.

"That dinner party at Crystal and Simon's is next weekend."

Despite her deliberately casual tone, he sensed the nerves beneath her words, and it was those nerves that let him hope that she might be getting ready to make the next move.

"Are you asking me for a date?"

"I'm asking you to go with me to a dinner party at my sister's house. Crystal doesn't like to set thirteen places at a table so she asked me to bring a date." She sent him a mischievous grin. "I thought I'd invite you instead."

"Ouch." He pretended in wince in pain.

"Are you interested in a free meal?"

"Always," he assured her. "Can I kiss you good-night at the end of the evening?"

She considered his question before finally responding, "Maybe."

Marcus raised his brows. "Maybe?"

"We'll have to see how the evening goes."

"When?"

"Saturday night. Seven o'clock."

He was already looking forward to it.

Marcus enjoyed spending time with Jewel's sister. She was outgoing and fun—and a valuable ally in his battle to overcome Jewel's reservations about getting involved with him.

"Has she invited you to be her date for my dinner party yet?" Crystal asked, when she caught up with him at the stable Tuesday afternoon.

"Yes, although that's not quite how the invitation was issued."

"What do you mean?"

"She asked me to go," he admitted. "Because if she showed up alone, there would be thirteen at the table and that would be bad luck."

Crystal rolled her eyes. "If that's the explanation she gave for inviting you, I'm surprised you didn't turn her down."

He shrugged. "I figure dinner at your place means you're making dessert."

"Black Forest Cake," she promised.

"Mmm." He hummed his approval before asking, "Who else is going to be at this dinner party?"

"Mostly business associates of Simon's," she told him. "Several of whom have some connection to the thoroughbred industry—as most people living in Alliston do. And Hugo DaCosta, one of Simon's oldest and biggest clients, is bringing a friend—a prince, he claims."

Mac stilled. "A prince?"

Crystal nodded. "Yeah. From some obscure little country in the Mediterranean."

He nearly groaned. Knowing that Cameron was in West Virginia, there was no hope that Crystal's royal dinner guest was anyone other than his cousin. Which meant that he had to find a way to back out of his date with Jewel, because there was no way Cameron wouldn't blow his cover, and he wasn't nearly ready for Jewel to learn the truth of his identity. Not until he knew that the feelings she was starting to have for him were real and wouldn't be influenced by his title.

"Have you met this guy—this prince?" he asked casually.

"No, but Jewel did. He was at the race in Arlington with DaCosta last weekend." She grinned at him. "Why? Are you worried that my sister will fall head over heels for him just because of his title?"

"I'm sure it happens." He spread fresh bedding in the stall.

"I'm sure it does," she said. "But not with Jewel. In fact, she specifically asked not to be seated next to him at the table." She winked at him. "Which is when I told her that she would have to bring a date to ensure that didn't happen."

Marcus lifted another forkful of straw and wondered how he was now going to extricate himself from a situation he'd deliberately maneuvered himself into.

He'd told Jewel the next move would need to be hers, and she'd finally made it. Now he had to change those plans—and he had a feeling she wasn't going to appreciate that at all.

* * *

Jewel told herself it was ridiculous to feel nervous. This was a business dinner at her sister's house, not unlike other events she'd attended there in the past. Except that this was the first time she had a date, and she couldn't forget the warmth in Mac's eyes when he'd agreed to come with her tonight.

Still, there was a part of her that wondered if inviting him had been a mistake. They were moving toward something she wasn't sure she was ready for yet didn't seem to know how— or even want—to avoid.

Which was one of the reasons she'd opted to run some errands in town and meet him at the house, rather than arriving with him. She figured there would be fewer expectations if they didn't show up and leave together. Or maybe she was just a coward—afraid to face her feelings for Mac, afraid to go after what she really wanted. Because she really wanted Mac.

She looked around for his car, but didn't see it anywhere on the street or in the driveway. She hoped he wasn't running behind schedule. As nervous as she was about this date, she was even more uneasy about facing Prince Cameron again without Mac by her side.

She was almost at the door when her cell phone rang. She flipped it open, her eyes scanning the street for any sign of Mac arriving.

"Callahan," she answered.

"Jewel—I'm glad I caught you."

She frowned as she recognized Mac's voice. "Where are you?"

"That's why I'm calling," he said. "I'm sorry to do this at the last minute, but as it turns out, I'm not going to make it."

"What is it? Is there a problem at the stables? Do you need me to come back?"

"No, there's not a problem." There was a slight hesitation, as if he wasn't sure what to say to her. "I'm sorry."

"You call me as I'm walking into my sister's house to tell me you're sorry?"

"I'm having trouble hearing you, Jewel. I think the call's about to drop."

And she knew then, even before the line went dead, that he was going to hang up on her.

Chapter Nine

Jewel was still fuming when she drove home at the end of the evening.

Not only had Mac stood her up, but he'd lied to her.

The only good thing to transpire from the evening was that Prince Cameron had kept his hands to himself—although the fact that he was seated on the opposite side of the table might have had something to do with that—and agreed to come out to the farm to discuss with her *and* Caleb the training of a two-year-old he was in negotiations to buy. Her anger at Mac was pushed aside for a moment as she considered the possibility that the royal might choose CTC to train the promising colt he'd recently purchased. It would be a coup for the business—and a relief to her personally. If she had the sought-after chestnut colt in her stable, it wouldn't matter what Gabe Anderson chose to do with his horses.

But her focus—and her fury—swung right back to Mac Delgado when she pulled into the long, winding driveway toward home. She didn't care that he'd changed his mind about going to Crystal's dinner party, she just wished he'd had the decency to let her know five minutes *before* she was on the verge of walking into the door of her sister's house. And she absolutely wouldn't tolerate being lied to.

As angry as she was, she knew it would be smart to wait until morning to confront him, but her emotions were too churned to be rational. So she parked her truck beside the house and stormed across the yard to the apartments above the stables.

There was no response to her knock on his door, a fact which only fuelled her anger. Maybe he'd gotten a better offer—a chance for a "real" date and everything that might entail. Her stomach twisted at the thought. Of course, he had every right to go out, to date whoever he wanted. She had no claim on him, nor did she want one.

She was just furious—more at herself than Mac. She'd actually started to think she could trust him, which only proved that she was a fool. How many times did she have to be let down before she finally learned that there was no one she could count on?

She stormed back to the house and up to her room, where she kicked off her shoes and yanked her dress over her head. She tossed it toward the chair, not caring when it landed in a puddle of crimson silk on the floor. Then she tugged on a pair of jeans and T-shirt and headed back outside. If she couldn't kick Mac Delgado's ass, she could at least work off some of her bad mood down at the stables.

She went directly to Cayenne's stall. Jewel had been so busy with other responsibilities that the spirited stallion had been sorely neglected over the past few days, and with a prospective buyer in the wings, she couldn't allow that to happen.

It was Mac, she remembered now, who had directed Harold Emerson's attention to Cayenne. Mac who had made the man look beyond the horse's reputation to see his beauty and potential. She could acknowledge that fact and be grateful to him for it—but it didn't make her any less mad at him.

She came to an abrupt halt outside of Cayenne's stall. Cayenne's *empty* stall. She turned around, checking the stall across from his. Mystic stared back at her, head bobbing in acknowledgment of her presence. Jewel gave the aging mare an absent pat before she retraced her steps, checking every stall, as if someone might have simply misplaced a twelve-hundred-pound animal.

She then went outside to check the paddocks, hoping he'd just been forgotten outside. She would certainly reprimand the student who had been in charge of ensuring the animals were bedded down for the night, but so long as Cayenne was safe, there was no real harm done.

Except he wasn't in the paddock.

But from her vantage point behind the stable, she could see the lights on in the arena. She should have spotted them when she'd made her way to the Haven stable, but she'd been so preoccupied with her anger at Mac that she hadn't been paying attention to anything else.

She headed toward the arena, relief surging through her when she found that Cayenne was, in fact, inside. And so was Mac.

His back was to her, allowing her to approach without

being noticed, though he was so intently focused on the horse she wasn't sure he'd have seen her even if she was in his line of sight. The fury and frustration that had bubbled up inside her when she'd spotted him there were tempered now by curiosity and confusion. She didn't say anything, not just because she didn't want to break his concentration, but because she wanted to observe without Mac knowing she was there. So she folded her arms on the top of the boards and settled in to watch.

Judging by the sheen of the horse's coat and the perspiration that dampened the back of Mac's shirt, he'd had the stallion on the longe line for a while. But Cayenne appeared to be resisting all cues, and yet Mac persisted. He wasn't harsh but he was relentless, not mean but demanding. And through it all, he spoke to the stallion, using a firm but level tone to indicate he was the one in charge. Whether Cayenne finally accepted that fact or Mac simply wore him out, the horse stopped fighting and let Mac run him through some basic exercises.

As Jewel watched, the last of her anger and frustration drained away leaving other more complicated feelings in their wake. She shook her head, wondering how he managed to do this to her, how one man could pull so many conflicting emotions out of her.

She didn't like knowing that she had so little control over her own feelings where he was concerned. And she especially didn't like that she felt things for Mac she hadn't felt in a very long time, if ever before.

She watched the muscles in his arms bunch and flex, noted the way the thin, damp fabric of his T-shirt moulded to his lean, hard torso. As she watched, her throat got dry, her knees got weak and her heart pounded. And she realized it was desire that stirred inside her now—hot and insistent and undeniable.

He drew the horse close, rubbed a strong hand over its long neck as he spoke quietly to the animal. She couldn't hear his words, just the low timbre of his voice, a sound that apparently soothed the strong stallion even while it stirred her.

He turned to exit the arena, and halted abruptly when his gaze landed on Jewel.

"How long have you been here?" he asked her.

"A while," she said. "You've made some progress with him."

He shrugged. "I'm not sure it's enough."

She wasn't, either, but the only thing that mattered to her right now was that he'd made the effort—and that the horse was responding to him as he hadn't responded to anyone else.

She fell into step beside him as he walked Cayenne back to the stable. He kept his focus on the stallion, checking him for signs of heat when they got back to the stable, sponging him down to wash away the sweat and refresh him and examining his feet for stones. Only when the animal had been properly cared for and returned to his stall did Mac turn to her.

"I'm sorry for canceling at the last minute," he finally said.

"Is that why you're here? Is this supposed to be some kind of penance for standing me up?"

He shook his head as he washed up. "I'm here because I knew you couldn't be, because we only have five more weeks before Emerson's deadline and with every day that passes, I'm more certain it isn't enough time."

She wondered at his use of the term "we." They *had* been working together a lot at Haven and she knew he genuinely cared about the animals. But she'd thought he cared about her, too, as she was starting to care about him. She'd thought inviting him to the dinner party at her sister's house would show him that she was finally ready to acknowledge her growing attraction to him.

Either he hadn't understood the magnitude of that step for her, or it just hadn't mattered to him. Regardless, the mistake had been her own.

When would she learn? When would she realize the folly of opening up her heart to men who wanted no part of it?

She pushed aside her hurt and disappointment and said, "I appreciate your efforts."

"But you're still mad," he guessed.

"I was mad," she admitted. "Now I'm not entirely sure what I'm feeling."

He took a step closer and brushed his knuckles down her cheek. "Let me make it up to you."

The sincerity in his tone, the tenderness of the gesture, had her resolve weakening again. "There's no need."

"It's not about needing—" his hand dropped to her shoulder, then stroked down her arm from shoulder to wrist, and his fingers linked with hers "—but wanting."

He was holding her hand, but it was the desire in his eyes that held her spellbound. "Are we still talking about our date that didn't happen tonight?"

"The night's not over."

She swallowed. "But it's late."

"Not too late, I hope."

"Mac—"

"Why did you invite me to dinner tonight?"

She'd already told him why, though her explanation about the number of guests at the table hadn't been the real reason.

She could recite that same excuse now, or she could take a chance and tell him the truth. Except that she'd just finished berating herself for putting her heart on the line too many times in the past, and if she told him the truth now, wouldn't that just give him the power to hurt her again? Or would it give her the opportunity to experience something new and exciting, the possibility of which tempted her every time he was near?

"Because I've been thinking about you a lot lately. And not just in reference to the work you've been doing with the horses."

She saw the flicker of surprise in his eyes and knew he hadn't expected such a candid admission. They'd been dancing around the attraction for weeks now, and every time he'd taken a step forward, she'd taken two in retreat.

"I think about you all the time." His lips curved upward, just a little. "And rarely do my thoughts have anything to do with horses."

Her heart pounded harder, faster, urging her to forget about logic and reason and go after what she really wanted. "I've been thinking about sleeping with you."

It wasn't surprise that flickered in his eyes now, but desire that flared, searing her with intense heat that made her wonder how she had resisted him for so long—*why* she had resisted him for so long.

"How much longer till you get past the 'thinking' part?" he asked.

She took another step. She splayed her hands on his chest, and felt the thunderous beating of his heart beneath her palms. "About thirty seconds."

"Thirty seconds?"

Her hands slid upward to link behind his head.

"Give or take," she said, and pulled his mouth down to hers.

* * *

Mi Dios—the woman knew how to kiss. And like everything else Jewel did, she poured her heart and soul into it. He tasted her passion—and the promise of more. And the flavor—*her* flavor—was so tempting and intoxicating, it made him dizzy with wanting.

More. He murmured the word against her lips and drew her closer. She gave him more. More than he'd thought was possible from a kiss. And more than he had a right to take.

When he'd canceled their plans earlier, he'd known she would be annoyed, angry even, and he'd told himself it was for the best. He was only going to be in town a few more weeks, and though he'd never promised any woman more than that, he'd wished he could give her more. And it was the wishing that warned him he was already in too deep.

He couldn't risk falling in love. It wasn't something he'd ever worried about before, because he'd never met another woman who made him feel and want so much. In fact, he'd started to wonder if he was simply incapable of that emotion, if he might never fall in love. Then he'd met Jewel, and he'd been off balance ever since.

Which was exactly why he'd believed he'd done the right thing in canceling their date. There was no point in starting a relationship with Jewel when there could be no future for them together. Though he had no doubt that both of them would be extremely satisfied if he took her to his bed, doing so with so many secrets still between them would only end up hurting her in the end.

He didn't want to hurt her, though he knew he'd done so tonight. He couldn't tell her why he'd stood her up. He couldn't explain why he'd stayed away when he'd wanted nothing more than to be by her side. And even if he tried, he wasn't sure she'd believe him.

But as her lips parted and her body pressed closer, he realized she'd forgiven him. Or maybe it was just that, at the moment, she didn't care. As, at the moment, he was having trouble caring about anything but the willingness of the woman in his arms.

He'd wanted her from the first minute he set eyes on her, and with each day that he'd been at the farm, the wanting had grown. But what he'd accepted as a basic and primal desire—no different than what he'd felt for other women before—had somehow changed over the past few weeks. Into something deeper, dangerous.

She eased her lips from his, and when her eyes opened, they were dark and clouded with desire. "Come up to the house with me, Mac."

He was torn between taking what he wanted and doing what was right, between what he needed and what was wise. His body urged him to accept what she was offering before she had a change of heart, his mind warned him that it would be a mistake to let himself get involved any deeper, and his heart worried that she deserved more than he could ever give her.

"I've been working all day," he warned her.

"I know."

She was nearly a foot shorter than he, yet somehow she fit perfectly in his arms. She was warm and soft and fragrant—and he was hot and smelled like horses, if not worse. "I'm sweaty."

She nipped at his bottom lip, tugging playfully on it with her teeth. Blood pounded through his veins, in his head, blocking out all thought and reason.

"I'm hoping we'll both be even sweatier before we're done," she told him.

It would take a stronger man than he to resist a woman he'd wanted so much and for so long, and he gave up the pretense of even trying. "I'll race you to the house."

She pulled out of his arms and took off running. He chased after her, letting her keep the lead until they were almost at the back porch, then he caught her around the waist and pulled her back against him.

"Not a bad effort—for a girl," he teased.

She tilted her head back, her eyes narrowed. "I would think, at least right now, you would appreciate the fact that I'm female."

"Believe me—" he brushed his lips over hers "—I'm appreciative."

She pushed open the door and led him inside.

"Bedroom?" he asked.

"Upstairs." She reached for his hand, but he reached for her, scooping her into his arms.

Jewel let out a breathless laugh as he took the stairs two at a time. "I really love a strong man."

"And I love a willing woman," he said, tumbling onto the bed with her.

She gloried in the weight of his hard body against hers, the thrill of those talented hands moving over her, the pleasure of his avid mouth sampling hers.

Her mind blurred, her body yearned. She was more than ready to stop thinking and start doing.

But while she was eager to move things along, Mac seemed determined to draw out the experience, savor the moment.

He spoke softly to her. There was more than the hint of a

Spanish accent now—he was speaking fluently in the language, a fact that might have puzzled her if she wasn't so aroused. She could barely hear the words, never mind understand them, yet the sensual tone sent shivers of anticipation dancing over her skin. She hadn't expected romance, didn't need seduction. But with every pass of his hands, every brush of his lips, he patiently and thoroughly seduced not just her body but her heart and her soul.

"Mac." His name was a whisper, a plea, though she wasn't entirely sure what she was asking of him.

But he was, and while he still didn't rush, he did—finally—strip away their clothes. First hers, then his own. Then they were naked together, and the heat of his skin against hers, all those wonderfully taut muscles at her fingertips, was almost more than she could stand.

She moaned in sensual pleasure as his tongue slipped into her mouth, and she instinctively arched against him, silently pleading for a more intimate penetration.

But he only continued to kiss her, deeply, thoroughly, endlessly. She responded to his kiss, learning the shape of his lips, exploring the texture of his mouth, savoring the flavor that was uniquely Mac. Though her experience was admittedly limited—and no doubt a lot more limited than his—she'd long accepted that kissing was a means to an end as far as the male gender was concerned. A starting point on the road to seduction, the enjoyment of which was forgotten in the push toward the finish as soon as clothes were shed.

But here they were, their naked bodies tangled together, and still Mac only kissed her.

And then he touched her.

Light, gentle strokes of his hands.

Lazy, tantalizing caresses.

As if he wasn't just discovering, but memorizing every dip and curve of her body. The palms of his hands weren't smooth anymore, and the scrape of the rough skin against her sensitive flesh was deliciously erotic. With each pass of his hands, the pleasure and anticipation built inside of her until she was quivering with need.

After what seemed like an eternity, his mouth moved away from hers, his lips trailing across her cheek to nibble on her earlobe, then nuzzle the tender skin beneath. She shivered and moaned, and his mouth skimmed down her throat, over the curve of one breast. His tongue swirled around the crest in a sensual journey that slowly meandered closer to the tight bud. He touched his tongue to her nipple, a gentle lick, a leisurely nibble. Then his lips closed over the aching peak, and she closed her eyes and bit down on her bottom lip to keep from crying out as he suckled and tugged. Sparks of fiery pleasure shot through her, accelerating the flames of a heated passion that was already burning out of control.

She wasn't sure she'd ever known such an intensity of need or experienced such a raging storm of desire. It was as if nothing existed outside of the moment, as if nothing else mattered.

"Mac," she said again.

He responded by shifting his focus to her other breast, giving it the same delicious attention and driving her closer and closer to the edge.

She wanted him—desperately. But she didn't want this seductive exploration to end. She wanted to discover every inch of him, with her hands, her lips, her body.

His mouth was moving lower now, simultaneously enticing

and tormenting. Her hands slipped from his shoulders, her fingers curling into the bedspread beneath her back as he continued to tease and tantalize every part of her body. His lips caressed her belly, his tongue dipped into her navel, his teeth grazed her hip. She trembled—with anticipation, desire, need.

He lifted her hips off the mattress and zeroed in on the ultrasensitive spot at the apex of her thighs, and she cried out in shocked pleasure as he drove her to the edge of oblivion and beyond.

Her body was still trembling with the aftershocks when he finally rose over her. His body pressed down on her, into her. He groaned; she gasped. He more than filled her—he fulfilled her.

She moved with him slowly at first, then fast, faster. Her hands cupped his taut buttocks, her hips arched to take him deeper and her legs wrapped around him. His mouth covered hers, swallowing her sighs and moans as their bodies mated and merged, moving toward the ultimate pinnacle of pleasure, and finally leaping over the edge together.

Marcus had thought about making love with Jewel, but whatever fantasies his mind had conjured up didn't even begin to compare to the reality. Had he ever known a woman who gave so much? Who was so openly passionate? Or who made him want so much that even now, when their bodies were still joined together after lovemaking, he wanted her again?

He disentangled himself from her warm embrace and went to the bathroom to dispense with the condom. When he returned, she hadn't moved a single muscle. Her body was naked, her eyes were closed, her lips were curved.

She looked sated and sensual and just looking at her had his body stirring to life again.

He grabbed another condom before he slid into bed beside her again. Propping himself up on an elbow, he gently brushed her hair from her cheek.

Her eyelids fluttered, opened.

"I've wanted this," he told her, "wanted you just like this, from the very first time I saw you."

She smiled. "And I worried, from the beginning, that getting involved with you would be a bad idea."

"Are you sorry?"

"No." She pulled his head down to kiss him again. "I'm not sorry."

"Good." He lifted himself over her again, slid into her slick heat, and swallowed her gasp of shocked pleasure.

The first coupling had taken the sharpest edge off of his need for her, this time, he was determined to show her a little more patience, a little more finesse, a lot more pleasure.

Chapter Ten

Jewel woke up alone.

She was more relieved than surprised by the realization because she wasn't sure what she would have said or done if she'd found Mac beside her this morning. While she wouldn't go so far as to say it had been a mistake to take him to her bed—how could she possibly regret something that had been so incredible?—it had definitely been an impulse, and Jewel wasn't usually the type of woman to act on impulse.

Of course, now she couldn't help but wonder why he'd gone. Because he didn't want anyone to see him sneaking out of her house in the early light of morning? Or because he'd got what he'd wanted and he was finished with her?

No, she didn't believe that. She wouldn't believe it. Not after the incredible night they'd spent together.

And yet, despite the intimacies they'd shared, she was

aware that there was still so much she didn't know about him. Too much she didn't know.

This thought plagued her as she showered and dressed and went through the motions of her day. She didn't see Mac at all, though she found him at the center of her thoughts far more than he should be.

It was late and she was doing a final check on all of the horses at Haven when he came into the barn. Her heart did that now-familiar skip and jump, and the heat in his eyes when he looked at her was enough to have her flushing from the roots of her hair to the tip of her toes.

"Is everyone else gone?" he asked her.

She nodded.

"Good," he said, and pulled her into his arms for a long kiss. "I've been thinking about doing that all day."

"Kissing me?"

He smiled as his hands slid up her back, drawing her closer. "For starters."

They went up to the house together and made love again, slowly and very thoroughly. And when their bodies were finally sated, he kissed her again. There was more than passion in his kiss this time. More than she'd expected—more than she was ready for. She'd decided that she would have an affair with him—there really didn't seem to be any way to avoid it at this point. But she hadn't wanted any more than that.

"I'm thirty-four years old," she said.

His lips curved and he brushed them over hers. "You really have to get over this age thing."

"I am. Mostly."

She couldn't speak to him of the feelings that were in her heart. It would serve no purpose to admit that she was on the verge of falling in love with him. He would be gone in a few weeks and she would go on without him. But she would always be grateful to him for the memories he'd given her, and she wanted him to know that.

"I wasn't pointing out the fact that I'm older than you," she continued, "but that in my entire life, no one has ever made me feel the way you do."

"Nadie ha significado tanto a mí como usted."

"You know it drives me crazy when you speak Spanish."

"Usted me hace loco con el deseo."

She looped her arms around his neck and drew his head back down to nibble on his lips. "I warned you."

He grinned. "Are you going to punish me now?"

She pushed him onto his back and rose over him. "You have no idea."

Visitors to CTC weren't uncommon. Jack Callahan was proud of the facility he'd built and had implemented an open-door policy to show it off. Jewel had never seen any reason to change that, although her staff sometimes grumbled about the inconvenience of having to give impromptu tours. But while visitors in general weren't rare, female visitors wandering around on their own were. The woman she spotted by the paddock with Mac early Tuesday afternoon was clearly solo, undeniably gorgeous and definitely flirting with him.

Jewel paused in the shade of the barn and watched as the woman leaned closer to Mac, putting her hand on his forearm as she spoke to him. Mac smiled in response to whatever was said, then whistled for the chestnut filly, who trotted over to the fence.

The woman's glossy, painted lips curved wide and she took her hand off of Mac's arm to touch Ruby's nose.

Jewel felt a twist in her stomach. She couldn't deny the surge of annoyance that rose up in her, but she refused to dwell on it. She might have let Mac Delgado into her bed, but regardless of her ever-growing feelings for him, she had no illusions that they were involved in anything but a temporary and strictly physical relationship. She had no claim on him, and she wasn't going to start acting proprietary and jealous just because they were sleeping together.

But she noted with satisfaction that he stepped away from the other woman, deliberately putting the horse between them. Or maybe it only seemed deliberate to Jewel, because she wanted to believe he wasn't interested in anyone but her.

As she walked past the paddock, his head turned toward her. When he smiled, she felt the now-familiar but still-frustrating slow and liquid yearning spread through her veins. She'd thought the intensity of the attraction would start to fade—had, in fact, counted on it. But after almost two weeks of making love with him every night, it still only took a glance or a smile and shivers of anticipation danced over her skin.

It was undeniably exciting—and a little scary. Over the past few years, she'd been so focused on CTC and Haven that she'd had neither the time nor the interest in anything else. She hadn't wanted or needed any personal involvements.

Then, suddenly, Mac was there, and she found that she enjoyed his companionship too much. She liked talking to him, riding with him, just being with him. But what worried her was that she was starting to count on him being there, because she knew that he wasn't going to hang around indefinitely.

Despite the way his smile melted everything inside of her,

she was tempted to keep going, to prove that she could. But he waved her over, and she found herself moving toward him, wondering if it was already too late for her to walk away.

"…you should talk to Ms. Callahan," Mac was saying. Then to Jewel he said, "Ms. Spring has some horses in Texas that she's interested in moving up this way."

Jewel would bet that wasn't all the woman was interested in, but she forced a smile and offered her hand, noting the glint of rings and painted nails on the other woman's slender fingers.

"J.C. Callahan," she said. "And I promise, you won't find a better facility than ours anywhere in the state."

"J.C.?" The woman's exotic violet-colored eyes widened. "Oh, my goodness. It *is* you."

Now Jewel felt at even more of a disadvantage because, aside from Mac's reference to her as "Ms. Spring," she had no memory of having met her before.

"It's Natasha," she continued. "Formerly Natasha Kenesky. I grew up down the street—you used to babysit me."

The name clicked, and Jewel worked to keep her smile in place as she nodded. She remembered now, though the memory she had of nine-year-old "Nat" with pigtails and scraped knees bore little resemblance to the stunning beauty before her now. She was dressed casually for a visit to the farm, but her slim-fitting jeans and scoop-necked T-shirt bore designer labels.

"It's been a long time," Jewel said inanely.

Natasha laughed. "Almost twenty years. We moved away when Daddy got transferred to Houston for business. I always wanted to come back to Alliston, but I married a Texan who hated to travel. So after the divorce, I decided to make the move on my own.

"Now it's just me and the horses." Her voice dropped a notch, though not so much that Mac wouldn't clearly be able to hear every word she spoke. "I never guessed how lonely a big house would feel with no one to share it."

"You should get a puppy," Jewel suggested. "The local shelter has lots of dogs who need a good home."

Natasha laughed again. "Maybe I will, once I'm more settled. At the moment, I'm looking to make arrangements for my thoroughbreds."

"Who's training your horses?"

"They were working with Duane Watters in Texas. He gave me a couple of names, Caleb Bryce and Evan Horton. I want to meet with both of them before I decide."

"I imagine Evan's at the track today, prepping for the race tomorrow, as Caleb is," Jewel told her. "But you're welcome to check out the facilities while you're here."

"That would be good," Natasha said.

"Why don't you give her a tour, Mac?" Jewel said.

Natasha turned her attention and her megawatt smile on the man next to her again. "That would be even better."

The look he shot Jewel was both puzzled and wary, but he didn't protest the offer she'd made on his behalf.

"It was nice seeing you again, Nat," Jewel said, then continued on her way to the Haven barn.

Marcus knew women, and he knew without a doubt that Jewel was ticked about something. Actually he had a strong suspicion that it was some*one* rather than something—a suspicion that was strengthened when Natasha Spring sidled closer.

He dragged his attention away from the subtle sway of Jewel's hips to focus on the woman she had left in his charge.

"Have you worked here a long time?" she asked him.

"A couple of months," he said. "But I can honestly tell you that I've never worked anywhere else like this."

"I heard Gabe Anderson has his horses trained here."

"He does." Marcus turned to her. "Is he a friend of yours?"

She wrinkled her nose. "He's a self-important windbag, but he knows horses."

It would be completely inappropriate for Mac to agree with her derogatory comment about one of the farm's biggest clients, but he was impressed with her perception. Her obvious flirtation aside, she seemed to be an intelligent and savvy woman.

This opinion was further enforced by her comments and questions as he guided her around the facilities. She wasn't a discarded trophy wife who got the horses as part of her divorce settlement, but a woman who truly admired and cared for her animals and was determined to ensure they had the best housing and training.

While he went through the motions with Natasha, his mind kept drifting. He'd never objected to the company of a beautiful woman, nor had he ever had difficulty focusing on the woman in his company. But as he walked and talked with Natasha, it was Jewel who was on his mind. Jewel who was always on his mind these days.

He'd been attracted to other women, even infatuated with some of them. But never had any other woman captivated him so completely. Never had any other woman been the first thought in his mind in the morning and the last before he fell asleep at night. Never had he known another woman who made him want her all over again even while their bodies were still linked together after lovemaking. Never had another woman made him think of the physical act in terms of making love.

"She's a lucky lady," Natasha said softly.

Marcus started.

She smiled.

"Do you think I haven't noticed how your gaze keeps drifting toward the barn?"

"I'm sorry if I've seemed distracted—"

"*Distracted* isn't the word I would have used." The teasing light in her eyes dimmed just a little. "My husband used to look at me like that—as if I lit up the room just by walking into it."

"I'm sure you do," he told her.

She smiled again. "It's a little late to try charming me—I've seen where your interest lies."

"Have you seen the tack room?" he asked, steering her in that direction.

"I believe that was at the beginning of the tour, which means I've kept you from—" she paused significantly "—other things...long enough."

"I hope we'll see you back here again."

"You can count on it." She offered her hand. "Thank you for your time."

"It was a pleasure," he assured her.

She started to turn, then glanced back at him. "Can I give you some unsolicited advice?"

"Sure, but I won't promise to take it."

"Make sure she knows how you feel about her, Mac. Don't keep her guessing." Then, with a last smile and a wave, she was gone.

Mac watched her go, thinking about what she'd said, and wondering how he was supposed to share his feelings with Jewel when he wasn't even certain what they were anymore.

There was no doubt that his emotions were a lot deeper

than he'd anticipated, stronger than he'd wanted, more intense than anything else he'd ever known. But even if this was love, there was nothing to be gained by telling Jewel what was in his heart. Nothing that could be changed. She had hired him on for three months, and he had to be back home shortly after that. The celebrations for the four-hundredth anniversary of Tesorian independence were already underway and the whole royal family was expected to be in attendance. Even if he forgot about his other plans and opted to stay in West Virginia for a couple more weeks, it would only delay the inevitability of their parting, making it that much harder to leave her behind when he went back to his life in Tesoro del Mar.

No, there was no reason to change anything—and plenty of reasons to take advantage of every minute they had together now.

Nearly two hours passed between the time Jewel left Mac with Natasha until he came down to the Haven stable.

Jewel had just finished a workout with Cayenne and she was concerned about the animal's inconsistent behavior. It seemed he would take instruction when he was in the mood, but his moods were fickle, and Jewel knew that she had to find a way to change that if she was going to convince Harold Emerson to take him home.

She was toweling off the stallion when Mac came into the barn. He didn't say anything at first and she hadn't heard his steps, but the air was suddenly charged with an electricity that alerted her to his presence. The awareness between them had been almost tangible from the beginning, and was heightened rather than diminished by their intimacy.

"What did Ms. Spring think of the facilities?" She kept her tone casual and light, her focus on Cayenne.

"She was impressed." He picked up a brush and began making circular strokes over the stallion's flank. "She wants to meet with Caleb, of course, but I think she'll want to bring them here."

"I've no doubt she will," Jewel said, not quite able to mask her irritation this time. Frustrated with him, angrier with herself, she moved to the feed room to ready the evening meals for the animals.

"Why are you mad at me?" he asked.

She took her time measuring out grain. "I'm not mad."

"You don't sound not mad," he noted.

"I'm…annoyed."

"Why?"

"Only a man would need to ask such a question," she muttered.

"I am a man," he reminded her unnecessarily.

Yeah, she was well aware of that. As, she thought irritably, was any living, breathing female within a ten-mile radius. "She was flirting with you."

His brows drew together, though, to his credit, he didn't deny it. "That's right—*she* was flirting with *me*."

Jewel said nothing else as she worked her way from one stall to the next, automatically adding the required supplements to each animal's feed. Mac put Cayenne back in his stall and worked along with her, filling the water buckets. They'd established an easy rhythm of working together over the past several weeks, and only now did she realize how much help he'd been, how much she'd come to rely on him. And that worried her.

It was already the end of June—Grady's cast would be off in a few weeks and he'd be ready to return to work shortly after that. Mac had agreed to stay on until Grady came back, but she had no idea what his plans were beyond that. He had a life somewhere, she was sure of it. A future that involved some kind of corporate job with a big desk in a corner office, a secretary to manage his schedule and a girlfriend whose attention would be focused solely on him.

So why was he here? Why was he with her when he could be with someone unburdened by so many obligations and responsibilities? Someone younger and beautiful. Someone like Natasha.

She scowled at the thought as she shoved the scoop back into the bag. "I used to babysit her."

Mac put away the hose and wiped his hands. "She mentioned that. So what?"

"Let's just say it was a wake-up call."

"I'm sure there's a logical thought progression somewhere in your brain, but I'm not following it."

"She's older than you are."

"I'm still not following."

She shook her head at his stubborn refusal to see what was so glaringly obvious to her. "I used to babysit a woman who is now older than the man I'm currently sleeping with, which made me realize that if you had lived in the area as a kid, I might have been your babysitter, too."

He frowned at that. "It's back to the age thing again, isn't it?"

"Now you get it."

"What I get is that you're making a big deal out of something that shouldn't be."

"I graduated high school before you'd even started."

"How is that in any way relevant to what's happening between us now?"

She couldn't believe he couldn't see it. Or maybe he really didn't care because he was getting exactly what he wanted out of their relationship. "It highlights—at least for me—the fact that we're at different stages in our lives, that we want different things."

He slid his arms around her waist and drew her back against him, then dipped his head to kiss her neck, touching his lips to the ultrasensitive spot he'd discovered the first time they'd made love, and she couldn't help but shiver in response.

"I think our wants have meshed pretty well," he said, his breath warm on her ear.

She wouldn't let herself melt. She couldn't. But her voice wasn't quite steady when she responded. "Sex just clouds the issue."

His hands slid over her hips and down her thighs, caressing her through the denim. "Let's cloud the issue."

Those wickedly talented hands moved upward again, tracing her curves, skimming the sides of her breasts, stoking the fire that burned within her until she was aware of nothing but him, wanted nothing but him.

"How do you do this to me?" she wondered aloud.

His tongue traced the outline of her ear, his teeth tugged at the lobe. "Do what?" he whispered the question, the warmth of his breath making her shiver.

"Make me want so much," she whispered her response.

"What do you want, Jewel?"

She turned and lifted her arms to link them around his neck. "You."

"Well, that's handy," he said against her mouth. "Because I want you, too."

Her lips responded eagerly to his kiss. Her body yielded to

his. And her heart trembled, teetering for just a moment on the edge of something that was both tempting and terrifying before she yanked it back. She would gladly give herself over to the passion he evoked, willingly share the joys of making love with him, but she wouldn't let herself fall in love. Not again.

His lips moved across her jaw, down her throat. He nuzzled between her breasts, the coarse stubble of his unshaven jaw scraped against her tender skin and shot delicious arrows of excitement and anticipation zinging through her system.

"We can't do this." It was a weak protest at best, and they both knew it.

His gaze caught and held hers as his thumbs traced circles around the nipples straining against her bra. Her breath caught in her throat, his lips curved.

"I'm pretty sure we can," he told her.

His thumbs brushed over the turgid peaks and she had to bite down on her lip to hold back the moan as her brain completely short-circuited.

"Okay," she breathlessly relented. "But we can't do this here."

His lips cruised over hers again, savoring, seducing. "Let's go up to the house."

"Too far away," she said.

He lifted a brow. "You have a better idea?"

She just smiled and took his hand.

Chapter Eleven

Marcus stroked a hand over Jewel's hair, his fingers threading through those glorious silky curls that spilled down her back. And what a nice back it was, too—long and pale, soft skin over taut muscle. And then there was the delicious curve of her butt, and the endlessly long shapely legs.

He felt his body stirring and gave himself a mental shake. He'd only just had her and he wanted her again. But his desire for her was more than just physical, and if he let himself think about that too deeply, it might worry him. For now, he wasn't thinking—he was just enjoying the moment, savoring the sensation of her warm, naked body draped over his, the synchronicity of her heart beating in rhythm with his.

He'd never felt this kind of connection, this sense of rightness, with another woman. When he was with Jewel, there wasn't anywhere else in the world that he wanted to be.

Make sure she knows how you feel about her...don't keep her guessing.

Natasha's words nudged at the back of his mind. It was good advice, except that he wasn't entirely sure how to label what he was feeling.

Was this feeling of contentment and completion love?

How could he know when he'd never been in love before. Or maybe it was more accurate to say that he'd never let himself be in love. He'd always kept his relationships brief, ending his affairs long before either he or the woman concerned could start to think that it would turn into anything more.

He'd already been with Jewel longer than he'd been with any other woman, and still, he wasn't nearly ready to let her go. He wasn't sure he ever would be.

Of course, what he wanted wasn't really the issue. He was due back in Tesoro del Mar by the end of July to take part in the Independence Celebrations, and his participation in the scheduled events was a privilege as much as an obligation. But that meant he only had five weeks left to figure out what was happening with Jewel—and maybe convince her to visit his home with him.

As confused as he was about his own feelings, he was completely clueless about hers.

He knew the age difference bothered her, though he didn't understand why it should. Why did it matter that she was eight years older than he when there was such powerful chemistry between them?

But whether it was because of the age gap or for some other reason, it was obvious to Marcus that she was holding something back, and he didn't know how to break through the barriers she'd erected around her heart.

Even now, he had no idea what was going through her mind, though he was sure he could hear the gears turning.

"You're thinking again, aren't you?"

"Just about the fact that we actually did it in the hayloft." She shook her head, though the hint of a smile tugged at the corners of her mouth. "I haven't done this since I was seventeen—and even then, it wasn't anything like this."

He brushed a strand of hair from her cheek, then let his finger trace over her skin, following the curve of her jaw, the line of her throat. He loved touching her—the softness of her skin, the way her breath hitched and her eyes darkened.

"I haven't ever done anything like this before," he confided.

"Really?"

"Why does that surprise you?"

She shrugged. "I just figured you were a man who had been everywhere and done everything."

He frowned at the deliberately casual tone. "You don't think very much of me, do you?"

"Sometimes, I find myself thinking about you far more than I should," she said lightly.

"That's not what I meant, and you know it."

"Mac—"

"What I know is that you don't seem to mind sleeping with me so long as no one knows we're sleeping together."

She pushed herself up and reached for her shirt. "I just don't like the details of my personal life being subject to public scrutiny."

"Is that the real reason?" he demanded. "Or is it that you're ashamed of our relationship?"

"I'm not ashamed of our relationship—I'm just not entirely sure what our relationship is."

"Why can't we figure that out together?"

"You want me to be honest, Mac? The truth is—I don't trust that you'll stick around long enough to figure anything out."

"That's blunt enough," he said.

"Are you surprised?" She fumbled with the buttons on her shirt. "How can I trust you when you deliberately hold back from me? Anytime I try to talk to you about your family or your life outside of this farm, you sidetrack the conversation. Oh, you're good at it," she said. "So good that it took me a while to even realize you do it, but there's no doubt that you do.

"You want my heart and soul—and what have you given me, Mac? I don't know how you happened to show up at the café the day I was there, why you were even in town. I was so grateful you were there to help Scarlett birth her foal that I ignored my own questions and concerns. But you've been here almost two months now, and I still don't know anything about you. You haven't let me know anything about you."

"You're right," he said quietly, and noted that the confession had surprised her. "There are parts of my life that I didn't want put on display, but I wasn't intentionally hiding them from *you*."

"If not me, then from who?"

"Everyone else."

She sighed. "That's another one of those responses that seems to answer the question but doesn't really give anything away."

He tugged his shirt over his head. "My name isn't Mac."

She was reaching for her jeans when he spoke, and her hand dropped away. She looked up at him with questions and hurt and confusion swirling in the depths of her stormy eyes. "I thought that part, at least, was true."

"My real name is Marcus Andrew Charles," he said. "Hence Mac."

"Hence?" She shook her head. "I don't think I've ever known anyone else to actually use that word in a sentence. On the other hand, Marcus sounds a lot more Harvard than Mac." Her gaze narrowed. "You did go to Harvard, didn't you?"

He nodded, then, when it was apparent she was waiting for him to expand on that response, he added, "Law School."

"Oh." She blew out a breath. "Where did you get the business degree?"

"Management Studies at Cambridge."

"An internationally educated lawyer and a barrel-racer-turned-horse-trainer—talk about odd couples."

He wanted to tell her more—to tell her everything—but he wasn't sure she was ready to hear it, and he wasn't ready to lose her if she decided a relationship with a prince was more than she was ready to handle. So he only asked, "Why is that so odd?"

She shook her head. "I actually thought I was falling in love with you, Mac. But how can I love a man I don't even know?"

Four days after her argument with Mac—*Marcus*—Jewel was still feeling hurt and confused, still trying to figure out why a Harvard law graduate was mucking out her stalls and sleeping in her bed.

And yes, he was still sleeping in her bed, because everything else aside, she couldn't deny the connection between them was real. And if he was only going to be at CTC for a few more weeks, as they'd agreed from the beginning, she wasn't going to waste a single moment of that time. She also wasn't going to delude herself into thinking their relationship was anything more than purely physical and strictly temporary.

A knock at the door helped her push these thoughts from her mind, though the automatic smile she'd put on her face froze in place when she recognized the woman standing in the doorway. The last person Jewel wanted or expected to see in her office Friday morning was Natasha Spring.

"I just met with Caleb," Natasha said to Jewel. "And I have to say, I was really impressed with his ideas and philosophies. Of course, he wants to see my horses before he'll discuss the possibility of working them into his training schedule."

"That sounds like Caleb," Jewel agreed.

"So if it's all right with you, I'd like to make arrangements to have them sent up here, to be boarded and trained at CTC."

"How many horses are we talking?"

"Half a dozen."

Jewel nodded. "That would be fine."

In fact, it would be more than fine. It would help fill some of the stalls that would be left vacant when Gabe Anderson pulled his animals out, as she knew he was on the verge of doing.

"Great." Natasha's smile was wide and friendly. "There was something else I wanted to talk to you about, if you've got another minute."

"Sure. What is it?"

"Haven," the other woman said. "I have a lot of free time these days, and I was hoping I could spend some of it helping out at Haven."

"I can always use more help." And with the date of the annual charity auction coming up fast, she could use a lot of extra hands, but as she glanced at Natasha's perfectly mani-cured nails, she wasn't sure they were the right kind.

"But?" Nat prompted, sensing Jewel's hesitation.

"But I can't help wondering if you really want to help with the horses or you just want to hang around here to get to know Mac better."

"I really want to help out with the horses," Natasha said. "Considering my track record with men, I've decided to concentrate my attention on the horses for a while. Besides, as easy as Mac is on the eyes, I got the distinct impression that he only has eyes for you, and I would never poach on a friend."

"I have trouble reconciling the gap-toothed child I knew with the woman you are now," Jewel admitted.

"Does that mean we can't be friends?"

"No." Jewel stood up and offered her hand. "Welcome to Haven."

Over the next couple of weeks, Mac spent every free moment he had with Jewel, conscious of how little time they had left. Grady had stopped by the farm the day before, to show Jewel that he was mobile again and remind her of his imminent return to work. And when Grady came back, there would be no reason for Mac to stay.

No reason except Jewel, and as much as he wanted to stay with her, to be with her, he had his own responsibilities and obligations. Marcus was expected to be back in Tesoro del Mar along with the rest of the royal family for the independence festivities. And he wanted to be there—he just wished he could take Jewel with him.

There had been so many times over the past couple of weeks that he'd thought about telling her the truth about who he was, and each time, something had held him back. So many women had wanted to date him because of who he was—as if it was some kind of coup to be seen on the arm of a prince. He didn't think Jewel was the type of woman to care that he was royalty, but he was certain she wouldn't be pleased by his deception. And it was this certainty that made the truth stick in his throat whenever he tried to tell her.

Tonight, he resolved that he would find a way—until he saw the look of abject misery on her face.

He coaxed her to take a walk, and they ended up down by the stream. It was a beautiful summer night, warm and clear, and they sat on the bank of the creek. Jewel was cradled between his knees, her back against his front, his arms around her.

"Gabe Anderson gave me his notice today," she told him.

"I'm sorry."

"I thought I would be, too," she said. "In a lot of ways, though, I think it's probably for the best."

"It probably is," he agreed. "But I bet you still feel as if there was something you could or should have done to convince him to stay."

"He was angry that I backed Caleb's decision to scratch After Midnight from a race. I couldn't have done any differently. But you're right, I do wonder if I might have handled it better.

"It's a little overwhelming at times," she admitted. "Knowing that there are so many people—owners and employees— who are depending on me."

"Not to mention the horses," Mac added.

She smiled. "Though they're usually not as vocal in their displeasure."

"You're doing great work here—both with CTC and Haven."

"Cayenne is still balking at being handled by strangers."

He tightened his arms around her. "We still have a week."

She sighed as she leaned into his embrace. "Why does it seem there are never enough hours in a day?"

"Because you try to do too much for everyone," he told her.

"I just do my job," she insisted.

"Still, I wish I could take you away from here—for a day, a week, a month."

She smiled at the thought. "Where would we go?"

He pretended to consider the question for a minute before he said, "An island somewhere, where the sand is soft and white, the sky is clear and blue, and the waves lap gently against the shore." He felt a pang when he thought of it—both a longing for home and regret that his time here was marching inevitably toward its end.

She tipped her head back against his shoulder, oblivious to his thoughts, unaware of the realities of his life. "That sounds heavenly."

But of course she thought he was only spinning an elaborate fantasy for her. She had no idea that he could really give her everything he was offering—and more. And he was surprised by how very much he wanted to give her everything.

Was this love?

The question had been nagging at the back of his mind for weeks now, though he was still uncertain of the answer. And if he did love her, could he be lucky enough to find that she loved him, too? Maybe even enough to forgive him his deceptions.

"Let's do it," he said.

"Do what?"

He chuckled. "Go away together. There's an island in the Mediterranean—Tesoro del Mar. The name means treasure of the sea and I can honestly say I've never been to anyplace more beautiful."

"Tesoro del Mar," she echoed. "It does sound beautiful. And vaguely familiar." She frowned, as if trying to remember where she'd heard the name before.

"I'd love to take you there," Marcus continued.

"You're serious?"

"Absolutely," he assured her.

She sighed wistfully. "Oh, Mac. It sounds incredible, but I have responsibilities here that I can't just walk away from on a whim."

"You also have excellent staff who are more than capable of taking care of all the details if you wanted a break."

"I know they're capable," she agreed. "But I'm still the one who's ultimately responsible. I can't just run off into the sunset because it's what you want."

"What do you think I'm asking of you—a vacation on the beach with lots of sun and sand and sex?"

"Isn't that exactly what you were asking?"

"*Imbécil,*" he muttered.

She turned to glare at him. "I don't need to speak Spanish to understand *that.*"

He took her in his arms and pressed a brief, hard kiss to her lips. "*¿Cómo puede usted ser tan inteligente sobre tan muchas cosas y tan estúpido sobre mis sensaciones para usted?*"

Her brow furrowed. "Okay, that one I don't have the first clue about."

"You don't have the first clue about a lot of things."

"Meaning?"

He raked a hand through his hair, frustrated that she was making this so difficult and he was bungling it so badly. "Tesoro del Mar is my home," he finally said to her. "I'm asking you to come home with me."

Her eyes widened. "Oh."

He managed a smile. "I've never asked another woman to see where I come from, to meet my family."

"Oh," she said again.

"I have to go back at the end of the month, I'd like you to go with me."

"There's so much going on around here right now with planning for the auction and—"

He silenced her with a kiss. "Just take some time to think about it."

Jewel was able to think of little else over the next few days, and she was more tempted by Mac's offer than she would have expected. She'd traveled extensively throughout the U.S. but had rarely ventured outside of its borders. She'd been to Canada a couple of times—to Woodbine and Fort Erie, and to Mexico once. But she'd never been to the Mediterranean and the promise of sun and sand and some time alone with Mac was almost irresistible.

But the timing he'd suggested was less than ideal. Though Natasha and Crystal had happily taken the reins of the Fourth Annual Haven Charity Auction, Jewel wouldn't feel right dumping the whole project in their laps. Not that she didn't trust them to handle all of the details, she just wasn't used to relinquishing responsibility. After the auction would be better timing, and she thought she might suggest that possibility to Mac if he brought up the subject again.

Cody poked his head into Jewel's office. "There's a Prince Cameron Leandres here to see you."

Jewel managed not to groan out loud.

"He said you invited him to come by and tour the facilities," the young stable hand prompted.

"I did," she admitted, and reluctantly abandoned the papers on her desk to greet the prince.

Cameron scrutinized the lush green paddocks, the immaculate buildings and neat landscaping before turning to her. "I was just thinking the view couldn't get better, and then the sun suddenly shone brighter."

She forced a smile as she offered her hand. "I'm glad you were able to make it."

He took her hand and, as he had the first time, brought it to his lips. "Turning down an invitation from a beautiful woman is something I would never do."

"And I'm sure you'll find this visit worth your while." She pulled her hand from his and led the way to the main barn.

She looked up to see Mac coming toward her, and her heart did that funny little skip and jump that it always did when he was near. She smiled, not just relieved but genuinely pleased to see him, but noted that the light in his eyes dimmed when they landed on the man at her side.

She turned to Cameron, noted the sudden glint of what might have been satisfaction in his eyes, though she didn't have time to wonder about it. "Your Highness, I'd like to introduce you to—"

"No introductions are necessary." Though the prince was speaking to her, his gaze was on Mac.

She could feel the tension in the air and was suddenly filled with a deep sense of foreboding. "You've already met?"

"We have," Mac said shortly.

Cameron smirked. "Though I have to admit," he said, "that I didn't quite recognize you at first, Marcus. You look like a stable hand."

Mac's gaze slid to Jewel's, then away again. "Could I speak to you outside for a moment, Cameron?"

The prince shrugged. "Excuse me, Ms. Callahan, while I have a word with my cousin."

Chapter Twelve

Cousin?

Jewel stared. Surely Cameron had misspoken, but the flash of guilt in Mac's eyes assured her that he had not.

And suddenly she knew why the name of the island Mac had mentioned sounded familiar. Tesoro del Mar was Prince Cameron's home, and the prince and Mac were cousins, which meant that Mac could very well be some kind of royalty.

But he wouldn't have kept something like that from her. At least, she didn't want to believe he would, but she was no longer certain of anything.

The men had gone outside for some privacy, but Jewel found herself inching toward the door. Though she knew she might regret eavesdropping on their conversation, she had to know the truth.

"Why are you really here, Cameron?" Mac asked.

"I've bought a horse and I'm looking for somewhere to have it trained."

"How did you know I was here?"

"I saw you at Arlington, though again, I wasn't entirely sure it was you. This whole stable hand persona was quite a surprise. On the other hand, it really does suit you."

"You came here to stir up trouble because you're still pissed that Rowan's wearing the crown instead of you."

"I've dedicated my life to the people of Tesoro del Mar."

"You've dedicated your life to no one but *you*," Mac said derisively.

"It should be me on the throne," Cameron persisted. "Not your brother."

Jewel sagged against the door.

Mac's brother was the ruler of the country?

If that was true—and it seemed to be—then Mac wasn't some distant relative of the royal family but in direct line to the throne. And the only reason she could think of for him to have kept this information from her was that she hadn't mattered enough to him that he wanted her to know.

I'm asking you to come home with me…to meet my family.

His words echoed in her mind, taunting her.

What if she'd taken him up on his offer? Would he have told her then? Or had he never actually intended to take her to Tesoro del Mar or acknowledge the truth? Had everything they'd shared together—everything they'd meant to one another—been a lie?

She didn't want to believe it, but the sense of betrayal slashed like a knife through her heart.

She didn't hear any more of Mac's conversation with Cameron. She couldn't hear anything except the pounding in her head. Until the distant ring of a cell phone penetrated.

She managed to pull herself together and step out of the barn.

Prince Cameron, apparently having decided that he'd accomplished what he wanted to with respect to his cousin, had stalked off. Jewel could see him in the distance, talking to Natasha.

Mac looked at her—his eyes filled with regret and apology. He opened his mouth, as if to say something, then closed it when the ring sounded again. He yanked his cell out of his pocket, frowning at the display before answering with a terse, "Hello."

And then his face drained of all color.

Marcus heard the tension in his brother's voice and immediately knew something was wrong.

"There's been an accident," Rowan said.

And he was immediately transported to a different time and place, to another phone call that had started in exactly the same way.

He swallowed, but before he could even ask, Rowan continued, "It was a naval training exercise—or supposed to have been an exercise—and somehow Eric was shot."

Marcus closed his eyes.

"He's alive." Rowan's voice was hoarse. "But they couldn't give me any more details than that."

Alive.

Marcus clung to the word, trying to find both hope and solace in it. He couldn't face the possibility of losing another brother. It had been hard enough to accept Julian's and Catherine's tragic deaths, but his oldest brother had at least lived a little. He'd fallen in love, married and fathered three beautiful children.

Eric had never done any of those things. What he'd done was serve his country, not just willingly but happily. And now he was fighting for his life because of that service.

"Where is he?" Marcus managed to ask.

"He's being airlifted to Memorial Hospital in Port Augustine right now."

"I'll be there as soon as I can get a flight," Marcus said.

"Henri's on the other line right now making arrangements for a charter out of Alliston," Rowan told him. "I'll send you the details as soon as I have them."

"Thanks."

He disconnected the call, his thoughts filled with Eric. Memories of the times they'd spent together, the hopes and dreams they'd shared. Hopes and dreams that Eric, barely thirty-one years old, had never had a chance to realize.

"Mac?"

He blinked in response to her question, but it took a moment for his gaze to focus on her, another for recognition to set in.

"What happened?" Jewel asked gently.

"My brother." He swallowed. "Eric. I don't know all the details. Rowan said there had been an accident. He's being airlifted to the hospital."

He was in shock, and the realization had compassion pushing aside her own hurt and resentment. She touched his arm. "Do you want me to take you to the airport?"

He nodded slowly and glanced at the screen on his phone as a text message came through. "Rowan's secretary has arranged a private charter out of Alliston."

"It's only a fifteen-minute drive from here," she assured him. "Did you want some help to pack up your things?"

"There's nothing here that I need," he said.

And those words told Jewel everything she needed to know.

Turning away to hide the tears that burned her eyes, she said, "I'll go get my keys."

For the next twenty-four hours, Jewel was glued to the television. She watched the news, anxious for any information about Marcus's brother. Few details were revealed about the incident beyond the fact that His Royal Highness Prince Eric Santiago, an officer in the Tesorian royal navy, was seriously injured in a training exercise off the coast of Crete. A later update indicated that the prince was in recovery after a seven-hour surgery and his condition was noted as critical.

She hadn't heard anything from Mac, though she didn't expect to. Not only because she knew his thoughts would be focused on his brother, but because she'd sensed a finality in his goodbye before he'd stepped onto the plane that would take him back to Tesoro del Mar and out of her life forever.

When Crystal stopped by the next day, she found her sister inside the house, her eyes riveted to the television. "What are you—"

"Shh!" Jewel waved her hands impatiently to silence her, as the now-familiar photo of Prince Eric in his naval uniform appeared in the corner of the screen.

Crystal stepped closer, frowning at the television.

"—no change in the prince's condition this morning," the perky reporter announced, "but doctors remain optimistic. No statement has been released by the palace.

"In other news—"

Jewel muted the sound as Crystal sank onto the edge of the sofa beside her. "Was that...Mac?"

Jewel shook her head. "His brother, Eric."

"But it said…he's a…prince?"

Her sister's shock mirrored what Jewel had felt in response to Prince Cameron's big revelation the day before.

"Fourth in line to the throne of Tesoro del Mar," Jewel informed her matter-of-factly. "Mac—whose real name is Marcus, by the way—is younger, so he's fifth."

"Ohmygod. When did you find this out?"

"Yesterday. Just before he got the call about his brother's accident. I obviously forgot to ask about any royal connections when I interviewed him."

"I can't believe you've been dating a prince." Her sister's voice was filled with awe.

Jewel shook her head. "I was sleeping with a man who never told me he was a prince."

Marcus had paced the waiting room floor so constantly over the past four days, he was surprised he hadn't worn through the linoleum. But he couldn't tolerate sitting still and feeling helpless. So long as he was moving, he was at least doing something, even if it was only counting the steps—thirteen—that it took to get from one side of the room to the other.

"You've been restless since you got off the plane," Rowan noted dryly.

"I've had a lot on my mind," Marcus said.

"As we all have," his brother agreed. "But Eric's condition has been downgraded from critical to serious and the doctors have promised that he's on his way to recovery."

Marcus finally sank down into a chair across from him. "He'll live," he agreed, and they were all grateful for that fact. The bullet had caused some serious internal damage before lodging near Eric's spine. Surgery had been necessary to control the internal bleeding but it was also extremely risky. The tiniest error could have resulted in paralysis, and though the procedure was deemed a success, the doctors still didn't know if there was any permanent damage.

"The doctors aren't making any promises," Rowan acknowledged.

"They won't even guarantee that he'll walk again."

"Because they don't know him like we do. They don't realize there's nothing Eric can't do if he sets his mind to it."

Marcus nodded. "So he'll walk again." He made the statement as if it was already fact. "But his career will still be over."

"He has a lot of other options."

"Except returning to the navy."

And Marcus knew that was all Eric ever dreamed of, all he ever wanted.

He shook off the thought, because he knew he should be grateful that his brother was alive—and he was. But the whole incident made Marcus realize how quickly everything could change and had him looking more closely at his own life.

And somehow, thinking about what he wanted made him think of Jewel—and how completely he'd blown things with her.

Now that Eric's condition was no longer critical, his mind had started to wander. Mostly in Jewel's direction.

And he knew he'd never forget the look on her face—the shock, the disbelief, the disappointment—when Cameron revealed Marcus was his cousin. He could almost see the pieces click into place in her mind, and he could imagine the conclusions she'd drawn.

Of course, he hadn't had a chance to explain. And while he was certain Jewel would understand why he had to leave the way he did, he wasn't sure she would understand anything else.

He should have told her. He'd known that all along, but he'd been sure that he would have time to find the right words and the right moment. Then Cameron had shown up and everything had gone downhill from there.

He didn't remember much of what happened after Rowan's phone call. He knew Jewel had driven him to the airport, and before he'd boarded the plane, she'd squeezed his hand and whispered something like, "I hope your brother's okay."

He wasn't even sure if he'd said goodbye. And he didn't know if the tears he thought he'd seen were in her eyes or his own.

"Have you called her?"

Rowan's question jolted him back to the waiting room. "Who?"

His brother's brows lifted. "Do you really think I'm that clueless?"

"I don't think you're clueless at all."

"And yet, you still haven't answered my question."

"No, I haven't called her."

"Don't you think she'd appreciate hearing from you?"

"Right now, no. In fact, I'm guessing she'd prefer to never hear from me again."

"You blew it," Rowan said mildly. "That doesn't mean you don't deserve a chance to make things right."

Marcus wasn't sure Jewel would agree.

It had been a crazy few weeks, Lara thought, as she settled her eight-day-old baby at her breast.

Only a few years ago, she'd been alone. Oh, she'd worked for the royal family and lived in the palace, but she'd had no real home or family of her own. Now she was a wife and a mother, and she felt like she was the luckiest woman in the world. Not just because she was married to a prince and part of his family, but because she knew she was loved.

But it was Rowan's brothers who were on her mind now. Eric had been released from the hospital the same day she and the newest member of the royal family had come home. Though his injuries were going to require extensive physiotherapy and he would probably never again see active duty, he was alive. Less than three years after the deaths of Julian and Catherine, the possibility that the family might have suffered another tragedy—well, she couldn't even let herself think about it or she'd start blubbering again.

Rowan had played the part of stoic prince so well in public. It was only when they came home from the hospital at the end of the day that he would hold her close and she would feel him tremble, know how terrified he was of losing another brother. Only when they knew for certain that Eric would survive that he let himself cry.

She didn't know how Marcus was dealing with this latest crisis. He'd rushed home as soon as he'd learned of Eric's accident and had spent almost every minute with his injured brother. As prince regent, Rowan had duties to attend to that couldn't be put off even while Eric was fighting for his life. She had Christian, Lexi and Damon to care for as well as being in the last weeks of her pregnancy, so it was Marcus who had stayed at the hospital every minute that no one else was there.

Because he'd spent so much of his time at the hospital, she hadn't spent much time with him. But Lara could tell that he'd changed in the few months that he'd been away.

He'd always been the most easygoing of the brothers, the playboy prince whose natural charm and easy smile meant he was always surrounded by friends—and somehow still alone. But there was a new maturity about him, an intensity that she didn't think was solely the result of his brother's accident. Maybe it was because he'd graduated law school, maybe it was a natural maturation process, but she suspected it was something else—or some*one* else.

And while she knew it was really none of her business, she couldn't help wanting to help, wanting him to be as happy as she was.

Whether he would appreciate her interference or not, Lara resolved to find Marcus after she'd finished nursing Matthew and settled him down for his nap.

As it turned out, Marcus found her first. She was just buttoning up her top when he came into the nursery.

She shifted Matthew onto her shoulder, only to have her youngest brother-in-law scoop him right out of her arms. She felt a pang of loss and longing, her body's instinctive response to the baby's absence, but then she looked at Marcus cuddling his tiny nephew and her heart sighed and settled.

"Well," she said, "this saves me having to track you down."

"Why were you going to track me down?"

"To thank you for agreeing to make the trip to Ardena in Rowan's place." It wasn't her only reason, of course, but it was a valid one.

"It's just a goodwill visit—nothing I can screw up too badly."

Lara shook her head as she rose from the chair. "You always underestimate yourself—and the importance of what you do for your family and your country."

"I don't do much," he insisted. "Not compared to Rowan or Eric."

"You're younger than both of your brothers," she pointed out.

"The Aimless Heir," he said, quoting one of the less fa-
vorable monikers he'd been given. He gently rubbed his
nephew's back and touched his lips lightly to the top of the
baby's bald head.

The gesture was both easy and natural, and she wished
some of those nasty reporters could see the so-called Playboy
Prince now—looking like nothing more than the doting uncle
he'd always been to his niece and nephews. Of course, what
woman wouldn't melt at the sight of a strong, handsome man
cuddling a tiny baby?

"You're not aimless," she denied. "You just haven't found
your focus."

He settled in the rocking chair with the baby and smiled.
"You always did know how to put a positive spin on things."

"And you always managed to get exactly what you
wanted," she said. "So why have you given up this time?"

He rubbed a hand over the baby's back as he rocked. "Are
you talking about Jewel?"

"She is the reason you've been moping around here for the
past couple of weeks, isn't she?"

"I'm going to regret ever mentioning her name to you,
aren't I?"

"It was obvious, at least to me, that you were doing more
in West Virginia than taking care of her horses."

"I thought we had something really great going," he said.
"But she hasn't returned any of my calls since I got back."

"I've called every day for more than two weeks. I've
spoken with her sister, her housekeeper and her head trainer,
but I haven't managed to talk to Jewel."

"I don't imagine it occurred to you that she might not want
to talk to you?" Lara asked dryly.

"Of course it occurred to me," he admitted irritably, "but I didn't think she would hold out this long. It's been almost three weeks."

And with each passing day, he'd grown more frustrated, a reaction that had amused her at first. She'd thought that Marcus was annoyed at being stonewalled simply because it was a new experience for him, but she'd soon realized that he genuinely cared for this woman he'd left in America.

"You lied to her," she felt compelled to point out.

"I had to—she never would have hired me if she'd known the truth about who I was."

Lara nodded in acknowledgment of the fact. "But there was probably an opportunity later on—maybe before you slept with her?—that you might have let her know."

He sighed. "Yeah, I should have told her."

"Instead you let Cameron blow everything out of the water, not only blindsiding her but giving your cousin the satisfaction of screwing up your life."

"He certainly seemed to take pleasure in revealing my title to Jewel."

"Which he wouldn't have been able to do if you'd been honest with her."

He was silent, unable to dispute the fact.

She'd known Marcus for years and had never known him to be so captivated by a woman as he was by Jewel Callahan. Usually his interest peaked and waned in a predictable fashion, but there was nothing predictable about his involvement with this woman. It certainly piqued her curiosity about the American horse trainer who had her brother-in-law so unexpectedly tied in knots.

"Do you love her, Marcus?"

He considered the question as he carried the now-sleeping baby to his cradle and settled him into it. "I don't know," he finally responded.

And even if he did know, even if he did love Jewel, Lara wasn't sure he was ready to admit it—even to himself.

"Maybe that's something you should figure out before you pursue this," she said gently.

"I know I don't like the way things ended."

"But they did end," she pointed out. "As you knew they would. As she knew they would. Because you never made her any promises, did you?"

He shook his head.

Of course he didn't. Marcus didn't make promises. He didn't do long-term relationships and probably broke out in hives if a woman so much as uttered the word "commitment."

Lara didn't have a psychology degree, but she understood—even if he didn't—it was the pain of losing both of his parents that had taught him to guard his heart. The tragic deaths of Julian and Catherine would have reminded him of the dangers of getting too close to anyone, of the pain of losing someone he loved, and reinforced the barriers he'd already put into place.

But she suspected that somehow Jewel Callahan had managed to breach those barriers, even if neither she nor Marcus realized it.

"Can I ask another question?"

"Can I stop you?"

She ignored his sarcasm. "If Cameron hadn't blown your cover, if Eric hadn't been injured—where would you be right now?"

This time, he answered without hesitation. "With Jewel."

"Why?"

"Because I can't imagine moving on with my life without her in it."

It wasn't until the words spilled out of his mouth that he realized they were true. For so many years, he'd been searching for some direction or purpose without ever guessing that what he really wanted was some*one* to share his life with.

He was a prince, with all of the inherent rights and privileges of that title. And he'd never realized how empty his life was until Jewel filled it, had never known how lonely his heart was until it had belonged to her.

Lara smiled at him. "I think maybe you've already figured it out."

Chapter Thirteen

Natasha fairly danced into Jewel's office Saturday afternoon. "Guess who I just talked to on the phone?"

Jewel finished punching the last number in the calculator, then winced at the total she entered into the ledger. Since Harold Emerson had backed out of his agreement to purchase Cayenne—understandably, considering the way the horse had been acting since Mac left—and she'd had to repay his deposit, the Haven books had been in dire straits. Something was going to have to change—and soon—if they were going to continue to operate the facility as they were doing.

Tearing her attention from the book, she looked up at Natasha. The other woman's cheeks were pink and her eyes glowing with obvious excitement. "I'm not in the mood for guessing games," she told Natasha. "I have a lot on my mind."

"A lot?" Nat's brows lifted. "Or one man?"

Jewel dropped her gaze back to the keyboard. "Was there a reason you came in here?"

"Of course." The Haven volunteer lowered herself into the chair facing Jewel's desk. "We've got a buyer for Cayenne."

Her head jerked up in response to this unexpected news. "Harold Emerson changed his mind?"

Nat shook her head but her smile never wavered. "A new buyer—and an honest-to-goodness prince."

Jewel's excitement quickly turned to apprehension.

"Can you believe it?" Natasha continued. "One of the horses you rescued is going to find a permanent home in a royal stable. Just think of the publicity this will bring to Haven."

"Who—" Jewel had to clear her throat before she could continue. "Who is it?"

Nat glanced at the message pad in her hand. "His name is Rowan Santiago, prince regent of Tesoro del Mar." She looked up and shrugged. "I've never even heard of the country, and I don't know what a prince regent is, but royalty's royalty, right?"

Jewel knew, because she'd searched for information on Marcus's family on the Internet after she'd learned the truth about who he was. And she knew that Rowan was his oldest living brother who had become prince regent—ruler of the country only until his eldest nephew was of age to assume the throne—when the reigning prince and princess had died a few years back.

"Royalty or not," she pointed out to Natasha, ignoring both the knot in her belly and the ache in her heart, "the stables have to be investigated and approved before we can allow the sale to take place."

"Of course," Natasha said. "I told His Royal Highness as

much, and he said he would make the arrangements for your travel and accommodation at your convenience."

"*My* travel?"

Nat's lips twitched, as if she was fighting a smile. "Unless there's some reason you don't want to go to Tesoro del Mar."

It was a challenge more than a question, and though Jewel had never told Natasha that Mac Delgado was really Prince Marcus Santiago, it was obvious her new friend had somehow learned the truth.

"Is there?" Nat prompted.

"No," Jewel lied. "No reason at all."

As Jewel waited for her call to the prince regent to be connected, the knots in her stomach twisted and tightened. She tried to picture the prince's office in the palace, where he would be sitting when he responded to her call. Of course, her mind was a blank canvas because she knew nothing of palaces except for pictures of castles that she'd seen in fairy tales. She knew nothing of Marcus's life away from CTC. In fact, if there was one thing she'd learned over the past several weeks since he'd been gone, it was that she didn't know Marcus Santiago at all.

"Ms. Callahan?"

Jewel started at the sound of a lightly accented male voice on the line. "Yes."

"I'm putting your call through to the prince regent," the briskly efficient secretary told her.

Then there was another click, and another voice came on the line. "Ms. Callahan?"

"Yes," she said again.

"Thank you for getting back to me so promptly." The voice

was similar to Marcus's. Similar enough to make her heart ache, but not the same.

She swallowed around the tightness in her throat and forced herself to focus on the business at hand. "I understand you've expressed an interest in adopting a horse from Haven."

"I'm interested in a stallion known as Cayenne," the prince said. "I've heard good things about him."

"He's a beautiful animal, but he hasn't had an easy life and—"

"I know he's had some difficulties with training, but I'm confident we can work with him here."

"With all due respect, Your Highness, that's a bold statement coming from someone who's never even seen the animal."

"My brother has worked with him," he said. "And there isn't anyone whose opinion I trust more when it comes to horses."

Jewel was silent for a moment.

"Will ten thousand American dollars prove my interest in the stallion is genuine?" he asked.

It was an insultingly low offer for a horse of Cayenne's potential. On the other hand, it was ten thousand more than anyone else had been willing to pay and would go a long way toward putting her books back in the black—at least for a while. "You're offering to pay ten thousand dollars for the stallion?"

"No, Ms. Callahan, I'm offering ten thousand dollars to compensate you for your time and trouble if you will come here so that we can conclude our negotiations."

She sank into her chair, stunned—and even more wary. "You're going to pay me to come to Tesoro del Mar?"

"Consider it a contribution to your facility," he said.

"That's very generous," she murmured.

"And yet, you're still uncertain," he guessed.

"It's really not a good time for me to leave."

"I would come over myself," Rowan said, "but my wife just had a baby and I really don't want to be so far away from them right now."

She'd read about the birth, of course. Since Mac—Marcus, she mentally amended—had gone, she'd scoured the Internet on an almost daily basis for information about the royal family of Tesoro del Mar. So she knew that Marcus's sister-in-law had given birth to a seven-and-a-half-pound baby boy whom they'd named Matthew, and though no photos had yet been released of the baby, Jewel imagined he had what she now knew was the trademark Santiago dark hair and eyes, and the image stirred a fierce yearning inside of her for a child of her own.

"Fifteen thousand," he said, when she remained silent.

As his offer increased, so did her wariness. "Why are you so anxious for me to come to Tesoro del Mar?"

"I'm not sure if you're aware of it or not, but Marcus's birthday is coming up and, as he's spoken at length about this stallion, I thought he would be an appropriate gift for the occasion."

She wondered if the prince regent knew that she and Marcus had been involved. Maybe he didn't. Because she'd bet that if he did, he wouldn't be so anxious for her to come to the island. She could just imagine the scandal if it became public knowledge that the young prince had been sleeping with an older woman who wasn't just a commoner but a lowly horse trainer.

"When is his birthday?" she heard herself ask.

"The end of the month. Obviously that's one of the reasons I would like you to come over and check out the stables as soon as possible. The other reason is that Marcus is out of the country right now, so you wouldn't need to worry about crossing paths with him—if that was a concern."

Okay, maybe he did know about her relationship with Marcus. But Jewel found she wasn't bothered by the fact so much as she was relieved to find the last of her concerns eradicated. "If we agree on terms for the purchase of Cayenne, the fifteen thousand will be credited toward the purchase price."

"That sounds more than fair," Rowan agreed. "When can you come?"

She flipped through her calendar, knowing there would be some major juggling required regardless of the date she chose. But she figured the sooner the better, especially if it allowed her to make the trip there and back before Marcus ever knew she'd been in Tesoro del Mar.

"I could come Tuesday," she said.

"I'll make the arrangements."

Jewel spent the next forty-eight hours making sure everything would be taken care of at both CTC and Haven while she was away. The last person she told, and the person she most dreaded informing about her trip, was her sister. Though when she made the announcement, Crystal didn't even blink.

"Why aren't you surprised?" Jewel demanded.

Her sister's smile was indulgent. "Because you love the man. I can recognize the fact even if you refuse to admit it."

"I don't know what I feel for Marcus," she lied. "And my decision has nothing to do with him, anyway. In fact, he's not even going to be in the country."

Crystal frowned at that. "Where is he?"

"On a diplomatic tour of some neighboring islands."

"For how long?"

Jewel shrugged. "A couple of weeks."

"Oh." Crystal pouted for a moment, then asked, "Well, you'll go to the ball, anyway, won't you?"

"What ball?"

The question was met with a dramatic eye roll. "The Midsummer's Night Ball is Saturday night and it's the biggest annual fund-raising event for PACH—The Port Augustine Children's Hospital in Tesoro del Mar. Prince Marcus is a patron."

Obviously her sister had been spending some of her spare time on the Internet, too.

"I'll be home on Friday," Jewel told her.

"You should pack something appropriate—just in case," her sister advised.

"There won't be any 'just in case,'" Jewel assured her. "My return flight is booked, I have no intention of staying any longer than is absolutely necessary, and even if my departure was somehow delayed, there is no way I own anything appropriate to wear to a royal ball."

Crystal's brow furrowed. "You're probably right. Maybe you should borrow my midnight-blue Valentino gown. The one Simon bought for me when we were in Italy last year." She glanced down at her slightly expanded waistline. "I certainly won't be wearing it anytime soon."

"That's a generous offer, but I don't think I need a designer dress to check out the royal stables."

"I'm starting to think that ornery horse has more sense than you do," her sister grumbled.

Jewel took her sister's hand and squeezed it gently. "I appreciate what you're trying to do, but the only reason I'm going to Tesoro del Mar is to make sure that the environment is suitable for Cayenne."

"You doubt that it is?"

"No," she admitted. "But if I approve it without an inspection, it looks like I'm either ignoring the rules because the buyer is a prince or because I can't handle seeing Mac—Marcus—again."

"And even if that was true, you wouldn't admit it," Crystal noted.

"He's just a man who happens to be a prince, and even before I knew he had blue blood, I had no illusions about a future with him."

"I did."

Jewel raised her eyebrows; Crystal smiled.

"Not for me," she clarified. "But for you. The way he looked at you, I really thought—"

"He never promised me anything more than what we had," she told her sister. Then, she stood and picked up her suitcase. "I have to go."

"I hardly think the plane is going to leave without you."

"Maybe not, but I don't want to keep the pilot waiting." She kissed her sister's cheek.

"There's no harm in taking a week or two of vacation while you're away," Crystal called after her.

"I'll be back on Friday," she said again.

Jewel didn't know what to expect when she boarded the plane for Tesoro del Mar, and throughout the eight-hour flight, her apprehension continued to build.

She was still angry with Marcus and couldn't help but feel betrayed by his continued lies and deceptions. And yet, there was a part of her that desperately wanted to see him again, to be held in his arms just one more time.

She let out a sigh. It was a good thing he wasn't going to be in the country, because she wasn't sure she had the willpower to stay away from him. As upset as she'd been with him for deceiving her, her anger and hurt didn't compare to the emptiness she felt inside when she'd watched him get on that plane and fly out of her life.

She picked up the glass of wine she'd been served with lunch and marveled at the luxury of being the solo passenger on a private plane. She did a lot of flying, from one race track to the next, but she'd never even sprung for a first-class ticket before, so this was beyond anything in her wildest fantasies.

Except that in her wildest fantasies, she wouldn't be a solo passenger—Marcus would be there. And she knew now that dream couldn't ever come true.

She took another sip of her wine and tried to banish him from her mind, with as little success as she'd had over the past few weeks. She had no business fantasizing about a man who could never be hers, who probably hadn't given her a second thought since he'd walked out of her life.

Okay, she knew that was both untrue and unfair. Though she hadn't heard from him at all during the first week after he'd gone, she knew his brother's condition had been critical and she didn't blame him for focusing on that above all else. The day after Eric's condition was downgraded to serious, he'd called and left a message on her machine.

She hadn't called him back. She'd still been too hurt and angry then to want to talk to him.

He'd called again the following day, and every day after that for the next two weeks. She hadn't taken or returned any of his calls. As much as she'd longed to hear his voice, she'd managed to convince herself that it was best to make a clean break. It was one thing to let herself fantasize about the possibility of a future with him when he was just a young Harvard grad and quite another to do so after learning he was royalty.

She felt like such a fool.

She'd made a mistake when she'd run off to the rodeo with Thomas—believing she could be everything he wanted, as he was everything she wanted. But it turned out that she wasn't quite good enough. Just like she'd never been good enough for her father.

If she wasn't good enough for either of them, how could she possibly expect she'd be good enough for a prince?

The simple answer—the obvious answer—was that she couldn't. And it would be for the best if she just forgot she'd ever met Mac Delgado, never mind been foolish enough to fall in love with him.

Jewel met both of Marcus's brothers at the palace.

Eric, though currently wheelchair-bound, was in good spirits, and as charming and good-looking as his younger brother. Rowan shared both of his brothers' dark good looks but with an added air of maturity and a sense of contentment. It was readily obvious to Jewel that he was in love with his wife and infatuated with his infant son. As for Marcus's niece and nephews, she fell in love, hard and fast, with all of them.

But she was here to check out the stables, and after a casual luncheon with the prince regent and his family, Jewel was anxious to get down to business.

The stables were, not surprisingly, both impressive and immaculate, and Frank—who called himself a groom but seemed to manage the facilities—was gruff but charming. Within an hour of meeting him, Jewel was wishing she could take him back to West Virginia to work at CTC with her. Frank responded by offering her a job at the royal stables. In the end, they both agreed they would be most content staying where they were, though Jewel couldn't help remembering how much happier she'd been when Mac had been at CTC with her.

Marcus knew his visit to Ardena had been a success. He'd performed all of the necessary duties and attended all scheduled functions with a practiced smile, all the while wishing he was in West Virginia instead of western Europe. On more than one occasion, he found himself wondering how his brother managed the endless and often tedious responsibilities of his office without going out of his mind. But Rowan did so—and happily. And Marcus knew that his sister-in-law was primarily responsible for his brother's newfound happiness and contentment.

He used to believe that he was incapable of falling in love. He certainly never wanted to commit to a relationship with any one woman. And then he fell in love with Jewel.

He'd been fighting the truth for weeks now, certain that returning to Tesoro del Mar and leaving Jewel was inevitable from the beginning, that Eric's injury had only hastened his departure.

But so much had changed while he was in West Virginia with her, and he was no longer willing to accept that their relationship had to end. Rowan had fought for Lara, and Marcus was determined to do the same for the woman he loved.

But first he had to finish this tour for Rowan.

There was a morning newspaper delivered to Jewel along with a breakfast tray laden with everything from pastries and fresh fruit to oatmeal and eggs, a silver carafe of fresh coffee and an elegant cut-crystal vase holding a trio of cream-colored roses that she suspected had been snipped from the beautiful garden in the courtyard.

She was on her second cup of coffee when she opened the paper.

MIA Prince Back in Action.

The headline article was accompanied by a full-color photo of Marcus with a woman.

Prince Marcus of Tesoro del Mar enjoys a waltz with Princess Francesca at a gala reception held in his honor at the Ardena Royal Palace last evening, the caption read.

Jewel stared at the picture for a long time, as if to commit Marcus's face to memory when she already knew she would never forget a single detail. And as she absorbed every bit of the image, she could no longer deny that she'd fallen in love with him.

But just as there was no longer any denying that fact, nor was there any hope that their relationship could have ever been more than it was. He was a prince—and she was not a princess.

The girl in the photo was a princess. Not only royal but young and stunningly beautiful, and clearly besotted with the prince.

Marcus looked a little less enchanted by his dance partner, as if his mind might be somewhere else—or maybe that was only wishful thinking on her part.

She chided herself for the fanciful thought, knowing there was no way he could have been thinking of anyone other than the beautiful, blue-blooded female in his arms. And the sooner she accepted that and got back to the reality of her own life in West Virginia, the better.

She'd almost finished stuffing her clothes into her suitcase when Princess Lara stopped by her suite of rooms.

"I was hoping I could talk you into lounging around the pool with me for a while this afternoon," Lara said.

"Actually, I was just—"

"Packing?" The princess's eyes grew wide. "You're not planning on leaving already, are you?"

"There's no reason for me to stay," Jewel said. "And I can't imagine that Prince Rowan wants me hanging around here when the sooner I get home, the sooner I can make arrangements for Cayenne to be transported."

"There's every reason for you to stay," Lara argued. "Most notably that I've been overwhelmed by all the testosterone around here lately and am desperate for some female company."

Jewel hesitated for just a second, and the princess pounced.

"You'd planned to stay for three days—I really wish you would."

So Jewel spent the morning with Lara and the children at the pool. After lunch, the three older children had other activities, leaving the two women and the baby alone, and finally giving Jewel a chance to catch her breath.

"I don't know how you do it," she said.

"Do what?" Lara asked.

"Manage four kids without a nanny."

Lara laughed. "It was a matter of some contention between Rowan and I when I was expecting Matthew," she confided. "But what you may not know is that *I* was the nanny before I married Rowan, and I didn't want Christian, Lexi and Damon to feel that they were any less important to me because of the new baby coming along."

"*You* were the nanny?"

The princess nodded. "Going back to when Damon was still in diapers."

"I don't mean to be nosey," Jewel said, "but I thought a prince had to marry someone with royal blood."

"Every country seems to have its own rules regarding royal unions. Here it was that the bride of a prince has to be—among other things—if not of royal birth, then a citizen of Tesoro del Mar or France or Spain." She grinned. "But Marcus found a loophole of sorts—a legislative provision that allowed Rowan to marry me, anyway."

She stiffened automatically at the mention of Marcus's name, but the princess was gracious enough to pretend she hadn't noticed.

"And then, after we were married, he helped draft an amendment to the law so that a royal can now marry anyone who is, if not already a citizen of Tesoro del Mar, at least willing to become one."

Jewel didn't know why Lara was telling her any of this. She couldn't—didn't dare let herself—imagine how it might possibly be relevant to her.

"He talked to me about you," Lara said softly. "I've known him a long time, and yours is the first name he's ever introduced into a conversation."

"I think you're making it into something more than it was." As she'd done when she'd deluded herself into thinking that they'd shared something special, that she really mattered to Marcus. Then she'd found out he was a prince, and realized what a complete fool she'd been.

"Then you're not in love with my brother-in-law?" the other woman challenged.

Jewel shook her head. "My feelings aren't important."

Lara's gaze softened. "You know, I've been exactly where you are—in love with a man I didn't think could possibly love me back."

"I think this situation is a little different," Jewel said.

"Why?"

"For starters, we don't even live in the same country."

"That might require some creative juggling," Lara admitted. "But it's not an insurmountable obstacle."

"I'm eight years older than he is."

"Did that seem to be an issue for him?" the princess asked mildly.

"Not as much as it was for me," Jewel admitted. "And that was before I knew he was a prince.

"The thing is," she continued, "after I found out the truth, and when I had a chance to think about it, I was actually relieved he'd been called away."

"Why?"

"Because it gave us both an out—an opportunity to move on with our separate lives without accusations or recriminations."

"Or an excuse to avoid acknowledging your true feelings for one another."

"Whatever feelings I had were for Mac Delgado, not Prince Marcus Santiago."

Lara shook her head. "You're obviously well-suited for one another because you're just as obstinate as he is."

"We're not suited at all," Jewel insisted. "But I have some wonderful memories of the time we spent together, anyway, and that's why I have to leave before he gets back. If I see him again, if I let myself hope and believe that we could somehow work things out and that isn't what he wants, then I lose everything."

"What if he does want to work things out?"

Jewel's heart skipped a beat, then began to hammer furiously against her ribs. Because it wasn't the princess who had spoken. No, Lara was just sitting there, smiling, as the question came from somewhere behind Jewel, spoken by a deep male voice that was achingly familiar.

Chapter Fourteen

Jewel turned around slowly, and her breath caught.

Marcus stood behind her.

And seeing him there, so close she could almost reach out and touch him, made everything inside her weak.

She hadn't seen him in weeks, and she'd never seen him looking like this. He was wearing a dark suit with a snowy white shirt, paisley tie and shoes so polished she could probably see her reflection in them. He looked so incredibly handsome, and so very much a prince, her heart ached.

Lara rose from her chair, the baby in her arms. "I think it's time I put Matthew down for a nap." She stopped beside Marcus, kissed his cheek. "Welcome home."

He touched a hand gently to the baby's head and smiled at his sister-in-law. "Thanks."

"You can thank me by not screwing this up," Lara said, then disappeared inside the palace.

Alone now with the prince, Jewel didn't know what to say. The brief exchange between the princess and her brother-in-law confirmed that Lara was responsible for bringing Marcus home ahead of schedule. The fact that he hadn't questioned Jewel's presence proved that he wasn't surprised to find her there and probably already knew why she'd been summoned to Tesoro del Mar.

Marcus, too, remained silent, though his gaze moved over her avidly, hungrily.

"I heard you were in Ardena," she finally said. And because she'd known he was away, she'd made the mistake of letting herself relax, thinking she might actually be back in America before his royal duties allowed him to return to his home.

"Rowan doesn't like to be away from Lara and the baby for too long and Eric's obviously in no condition to go anywhere, so that left the onus on me to represent the family. Every now and again, I'm entrusted with the responsibility and sent off with fervent prayers that I won't embarrass the country."

"I hardly think that's a concern."

"Maybe not so much anymore," he acknowledged. "Apparently I've matured since I first went away to college."

"That happens sometimes," she agreed lightly.

"I don't think it was college that made the difference—I think it was you."

"Well, hanging out with an older woman might have an influence, too."

"Don't downplay what was between us," he said.

"What *was* between us—except a lot of lies and deceptions?"

"I should have told you the truth—"

"That would have been nice," she agreed.

"And the truth is, I've never felt about another woman the way I feel about you," he told her.

"Maybe because you've never before spent more than a couple of weeks with any one woman."

"You've been reading the tabloids."

She shrugged. "Well, you certainly didn't volunteer any personal information, and when you left, I realized I didn't know anything about you. I didn't know you at all."

"You do know me," he insisted. "My title doesn't change anything."

She shook her head sadly. "Your title changes *everything.*"

"Only if you let it," he insisted.

She managed a laugh. "You're a prince, Marcus. That's a fact that exists apart from all else."

"And that's exactly why I didn't tell you," he said. "For the first time in my life, I was with a woman who wanted to be with me because of me, not because of my title."

"And you thought that would change if you told me who you really were?"

"I didn't know."

"Then I guess we're even, because you don't know me at all, either."

"I made a mistake," he said softly.

She tore her gaze from his, afraid he'd see the yearning in her heart. "You don't fight fair," she protested.

"I don't want to fight at all."

"Why are you here, Marcus?"

"I wanted to show you my home and introduce you to my family," he reminded her.

"I've had the grand tour and I've met everyone already."

"And?" he prompted.

"It's beautiful," she admitted. "The palace, the island, everything. And your family is wonderful."

He settled his hands on her shoulders, and that simple contact had everything inside her melting.

"I'm glad you're here." His hands stroked down her arms to link with hers. "I've missed you, Jewel."

"I can't do this, Marcus." She couldn't let herself hope and dream, not again. Because she knew it would only be that much more painful when it finally ended.

"Do what?" he asked gently.

"Whatever it is you're asking of me."

"Right now, I'm only asking you to stay. Just for a while."

"I've left Crystal and Natasha with a ton of things to do for the auction and—"

He kissed her.

It was just a brush of his lips against hers, but it was enough to wipe every coherent thought from her mind.

It had been weeks since he'd touched her, kissed her, and though she was still hurt and angry about his lies and deceptions, all of that was forgotten in an instant—burned away by the heat of that contact, replaced by a soul-deep yearning.

"I know I don't have any right to ask," he told her. "But I'm asking anyway. Please."

He would beg. Marcus realized he was close to doing so already, but he didn't care. What was pride when she'd already stolen his heart?

But she didn't make him beg.

Instead she lifted her arms to link behind his head and rose up on her toes to kiss *him*.

Her mouth was soft and moist, and even sweeter than he remembered. He wrapped his arms around her and drew her against his body. She sighed and yielded.

The tip of her tongue touched his, a tentative stroke. He coaxed her to give more, to take more, and they both lost themselves in the passion of their kiss.

From the beginning, there had been something between them. A spark, a sizzle—he wasn't quite sure how to describe it. But over time, it had grown and deepened, and he was relieved to know that not even his betrayal had extinguished it.

When at last she drew away, they were both breathless.

"I want you, Jewel."

Her tongue swept over her bottom lip, erotically swollen from their kiss. "The wanting is the easy part," she told him.

He shook his head. "Wanting you these past few weeks, knowing you were beyond my reach—not just in physical distance—was killing me."

"Marcus—"

He laid his fingers against her lips. "Come inside with me. Please."

He saw the hesitation in her eyes, the caution, but she nodded.

He took her hand, linking their fingers together. He led the way quickly through the maze of corridors, partly because he was afraid she'd change her mind if he gave her the opportunity, and partly because he was just in that much of a hurry to be with her again.

Jewel barely had a moment to take in her surroundings— the antique carpet beneath her feet, the art on the walls or the huge four-poster bed that was neatly covered by a thick duvet and fluffy pillows before Marcus tore back the covers and tossed them aside.

But as soon as he laid her down on the bed, all sense of urgency seemed to vanish. His hands slowed and his lips lingered as he slowly stripped away her cover-up and then the scraps of material that comprised her bikini.

"Mi Dios," he breathed. "We would never have made it to my room if I'd known what you were wearing."

"I didn't bring a bathing suit," she told him. "So Lara had this one sent over from a local boutique."

He dispensed with his own clothes and knelt astride her on the mattress. "I'll be sure to thank her. Later."

Then he kissed her again, deeply, thoroughly. With his lips and his hands and his body, he brought her slowly but inexorably to the brink, and only then did he ease into her.

Her hands moved over his shoulders, following the contours of hard taut muscle and relishing the feel of warm tight skin as he pressed into her, giving and taking. She arched toward him, wanting and welcoming. They moved together, a perfectly choreographed rhythm that built toward a spectacular crescendo. His mouth covered hers again, swallowing her cries as she sobbed out his name.

He plunged one more time, giving himself to her, and everything inside her shattered.

It was a long time later before either of them spoke, and it was Marcus who did so first.

"You were wrong," he said to her.

Jewel was snuggled against his chest, warm in the embrace of his arms, and too contented to take offense at his words. "What was I wrong about?" she asked sleepily.

"The wanting being easy."

She tipped her head back. "It's not?"

"Not as easy as the loving." He brushed his lips over hers. "I do love you, Jewel."

Her heart—recently and not yet thoroughly recovered—tripped again. This was exactly why she hadn't wanted this—and exactly why she hadn't been able to walk away. Because she loved him, too. But rather than simplify things, it seemed to Jewel only to complicate matters.

"I don't want you to love me." Her voice was an anguished whisper. "And I don't want to love you."

He kissed the tears that slipped onto her cheeks, first one side, then the other. "But you do?" he asked hopefully.

Her arms tightened around him. "Yes, I do."

"I've had a lot of relationships," he told her.

"I know."

His smile was wry. "Not nearly as many as the tabloids would lead you to believe, but still a fair number."

"Why are we talking about this now?"

"Because more than one of my ex-girlfriends accused me of being emotionally stunted. Not that I believed it, but over the years, as one relationship after another ended, I started to wonder. Because I did date a lot of women, but I never fell in love with any of them." His lips brushed hers again. "Until you."

She sighed and melted into his kiss. "My life is in West Virginia. You understand that, don't you?"

"We'll work something out," he promised her.

She stayed for the ball, though with each day that passed, her trepidation grew. By all accounts, this charity ball was a big deal—there would be celebrities and dignitaries in attendance and a lot of media coverage of the event. But what made it an even bigger deal for Jewel was that it would be her first official public appearance with His Royal Highness Prince Marcus Santiago, and she couldn't have imagined being more nervous.

In the two days that preceded the ball, he'd taken her to the beach, to some of the shops in Port Augustine, the art gallery and the theater. While they were alone together, it was easy to forget his title. But everywhere they went in public, the press was close on their heels.

Jewel tried not to let the media attention bother her, but she wasn't used to being the subject of such scrutiny. And though headlines such as The Playboy Prince's New Playmate? were a little unnerving, the press really started having fun once her identity had been revealed and they could dig up all kinds of other information about her. Then the captions read The Prince's Rodeo Prize, Prince Marcus's American Mistress and, her least favorite of all, The Youngest Prince's Older Woman, which firmly negated his claim that no one cared about the age difference between them but her.

Still, Marcus didn't seem to pay much attention to the newspapers. He certainly didn't give any indication that he was bothered by what they said, but it wasn't so easy for Jewel to take in stride.

So when the day of the ball dawned and she learned that Lara had arranged for a hairdresser and stylist and a bevy of other assistants to help Jewel get ready for the event, she put herself in their hands. Willingly and gratefully.

The makeover was both time-consuming and thorough, so much so that she barely recognized herself when she was finally allowed to look in the mirror. Her hair had been piled high on her head, with a few curls artfully arranged to frame her face. Her makeup was flawless, highlighting her features without overpowering them. And her gown was Dior—a shimmering bronze creation that looked like something out of a fairy tale and made her feel like a princess.

Looking at the unfamiliar image in the mirror, Jewel could almost believe she was worthy of a prince—a thought that both excited and terrified her, because she knew the woman staring back at her wasn't real.

When Marcus took her hand and led her onto the dance floor, she couldn't help remembering the first time they'd danced, the first time he'd held her in his arms. On a scarred wooden floor in a country-western bar to tinny music playing from a jukebox. It seemed like a lifetime ago, in a different world, and in many ways, it was. Tonight, the floor was gleaming, the chandeliers sparkled and the music entranced.

But at the center of everything, at least for Jewel, was Marcus. He was dressed in military uniform, reminding everyone that he'd done his service in the army, if only the required two years, before he'd moved on to other things. Still, he was breathtakingly handsome in his formal attire. And he was, at least for tonight, hers.

As they waltzed slowly around the room, she was conscious of the many pairs of eyes that followed. She could almost hear the whispers and see the speculation in narrowed eyes.

"I feel as if everyone is looking at us," she confessed softly.

"Everyone's looking at me," he said. "And envying me because I have the most beautiful woman in the room in my arms."

She smiled at that, because she knew it was expected.

But his comment wasn't very reassuring. Sure, it was fun

to play dress-up and dance at a royal ball—or it might be fun if she could forget about all of the eyes focused on them— but she was so far removed from her life she hardly recognized herself.

"You look incredible in that gown," he said. "But you're just as beautiful to me in a pair of jeans and a T-shirt." His thumbs caressed her ribs through the fabric of her dress, the gentle touch causing sparks to skitter through her veins. "And even more beautiful in nothing at all."

"Marcus," she whispered his name, part warning, part longing.

His lips curved in a slow, sexy smile that was intended only for her.

The flurry of flashbulbs that went off proved otherwise.

She blinked and misstepped.

He smoothly executed a turn, moving her away from the cameras and allowing her to regain her composure.

"Sorry," she apologized.

"No need to be," he assured her. "You'll get used to the crowds and the cameras. Not to the point where you forget they're there, but enough to accept and pretend you don't mind."

"You've dealt with this your whole life," she realized.

"Not nearly as much as Rowan, especially since he became prince regent. I figure it's a small price to pay for the perks of being a prince."

And yet, she didn't believe it was. And she finally understood why he'd so carefully guarded his true identity when he'd been in West Virginia.

Jewel thought she would get a reprieve from the press when she returned to Alliston. She certainly never expected that the paparazzi would follow her back home. But that's exactly what happened, and it seemed she couldn't go to the store to buy a quart of milk without someone snapping pictures of her.

Still, it was more of an annoyance than anything. At least until one of the young colts at CTC started exhibiting symptoms of serious colic and Dr. Anderson, the local vet, couldn't get past the media vans that were parked at the end of her laneway. The vet ended up parking on the road and jogging down the mile-long driveway to the barn, by which time the colt's condition was so severe he required immediate abdominal surgery.

The colt was resting now, and Dr. Anderson was optimistic, but the owner was furious and Jewel couldn't blame him.

She was furious, too. At the parasitic press who were camped out in her driveway, and—irrational though she knew it was—at Marcus, too.

It was one thing to put up with the media spotlight when they were together—she could put up with almost anything when she was with him. But she didn't know how to handle any of this on her own, she didn't want to handle it on her own. She didn't *want* to live her life long-distance from the man she loved. And as much as she did love him, she couldn't do this. Not anymore.

The Independence Celebrations had finally concluded, and while Marcus had enjoyed participating in all of the festivities and especially the time he'd spent with his family, he was glad that everything was done so he could go back to West Virginia and be with Jewel again. He'd missed her terribly over the past few weeks and it was only the knowledge that he would be seeing her again soon that got him through the long days and longer nights without her.

He was packing for his trip when the phone rang. A quick glance at the display revealed Jewel's number, and he was smiling when he connected the call. But his smile quickly faded when she told him about the colicky colt and how close she'd come to losing him.

He could hear the tears in her voice, knew she was fighting against them. But what worried him more was the niggling suspicion that she was upset about more than just a close call with one of her animals.

"I'll be there tomorrow," he promised her. "We'll get an injunction to keep the media—"

"No," she interrupted.

"Why not?"

"Because I don't want you here, Marcus."

It was her tone even more than the words that had everything inside him go cold. "You don't mean that."

"I do mean it. I can't live my life under a microscope, and being a prince, you don't have any choice except to live your life that way."

"I know the media attention has been a little intense—"

"Don't try and downplay what happened here. I'm not complaining about a zealous photographer taking my picture on a bad hair day," she interrupted. "I'm talking about the fact that an animal almost died because the damn media vans were blocking the driveway so the vet couldn't get through."

"Let me make some calls," he said. "We'll get a restraining order—"

"No," she interrupted. "A restraining order might keep them off my property, but it will also fuel interest and speculation."

"I'm sorry, Jewel. I know this had been difficult."

"Sorry doesn't change anything," she said softly. "But at

least the press will lose interest in me when they know we're not together anymore."

And before he could say anything else, she'd broken the connection.

Eric figured if anyone had a right to be cranky and miserable, it was him. After all, he was the one with a cast on his leg and question marks in his future. But it was his little brother who was cleaning the floor with his chin, and who had been doing so for days. Though right now they were in the media room, sharing a bowl of pretzels and a couple of cold beers while a rugby game played out on the television.

"So you got dumped," he said unsympathetically. "It can't be the first time."

Marcus raised his eyebrows.

"Or maybe it is," Eric allowed. "In which case, it was long overdue."

"You're not seriously going to try to give me dating advice, are you?"

"I wouldn't dream of it," he said dryly.

"Good."

"I was actually just wondering if you were really over her," Eric said. "Because if you are, I thought I might take a trip to West Virginia when I get this cast off my leg."

"Only if you want both of them broken," Marcus muttered.

Eric lifted his bottle to his lips to hide his grin. "Okay, maybe that's a little tacky. I just figured she seemed to like you well enough, and people often said we could pass for twins."

"Except that you're dutiful and I'm charming," his brother reminded him.

"No one's seen much evidence of that infamous charm

lately," Eric pointed out. "In fact, you've been more tempera-mental than that stallion Rowan brought over from America."

Marcus ignored him, though his scowl darkened.

"On the other hand, she wasn't really any different than any of the other women you've dated over the years," he commented idly. "I mean, it's not like you planned to marry her or anything, right?"

Instead of going pale at the thought, as the Marcus of old would have done at the mere mention of marriage, his brother just continued to stare straight ahead. And that was when Eric realized how serious Marcus really was about Jewel, and that he wasn't just moping, he was nursing a broken heart.

The realization stirred his sympathies, but Eric knew that it was a brother's job to rub salt in the wounds—and though he knew it might be painful for Marcus now, it was also necessary to prod him to action.

"For what it's worth—not that I'm giving you advice, I'm just offering my two cents—I think you're doing the right thing. Chasing after a woman can never lead to anything but trouble."

"Thanks, Dear Abby." Marcus pushed to his feet. "On that note, I'm going down to the stables."

"Don't let that horse kick you when you're down," Eric called after him.

He was still grinning when Rowan came into the room.

"What did you say to set Marcus off?" he asked.

Eric shrugged. "I simply agreed that he'd done the right thing in ending his relationship with Jewel."

His older brother frowned. "You can't believe that—he's obviously miserable without her."

"Of course, I don't believe it," he agreed. "But I know the surest way to get Marcus to do something is—"

"—to tell him not to," Rowan finished with him.

Eric nodded.

Rowan eyed him with new respect. "And I always thought Marcus was the smart one."

"Marcus is the good-looking one. *I'm* the smart one."

Rowan chuckled at that, but then he asked, "Which one am I?"

"You were always the responsible one."

His brother winced. "I guess I asked for that."

"You were the one we looked up to," Eric explained to him. "The one who instinctively did the right thing—as you did when you left London to come home and raise Julian and Catherine's kids. Of course, we changed your moniker when you married Lara."

"To what?" Rowan asked warily.

"The lucky one."

Rowan smiled. "You're right on that one," he said. "Because not a day has gone by since Lara and I exchanged vows that I haven't thought about how fortunate I am."

"Because you fell in love?"

"Because she loves me back."

And that, Eric knew, was truly lucky. Just as he knew that Marcus was on the verge of finding the same happiness—if only he was smart enough to grab hold of it with both hands.

As for himself, well, Eric was going to take that one step at a time. As soon as he was able to get back up on his feet again.

Chapter Fifteen

Jewel had asked Marcus not to come to West Virginia. She'd told him in no uncertain terms that their relationship was over, so there was no reason for her to feel so dejected and miserable just because he'd complied with her wishes. No reason at all except that she missed him. And with every day that passed, she missed him more.

She tried to fill her days with work, but not even that succeeded in keeping him from her thoughts. Every morning when she woke, she wondered where he was and what he was doing. And every night when she went to bed, she wished only that he was beside her.

Bonnie was unsympathetic to her moods; Crystal and Natasha were even worse. So Jewel kept her unhappiness and her heartache to herself. Mostly, anyway.

It was Wednesday, ten days before the Fourth Annual

Haven Charity Auction, when Crystal dropped a copy of the local newspaper on her desk. It was folded open to an ad for the event, and as her eyes skimmed the details, her heart pounded harder in her chest.

"Why does this say that Prince Marcus Santiago will be in attendance?"

Her sister frowned. "Didn't Natasha go over the draft press release with you?"

She'd wanted to, Jewel remembered now. Shortly after she'd returned from Tesoro del Mar, but Jewel had been more than a little distracted at the time, wallowing in her misery, and assured Natasha that she had free rein with respect to the ad campaign.

"We'll have to get the paper to print a correction," she said now.

"Why?" Crystal demanded.

"Because he's not coming."

"Actually, I am."

Jewel's heart skipped a beat, then raced, as she drew in a deep breath before she swiveled in her chair to face the man himself, standing in the doorway. "You have a bad habit of dropping into the middle of conversations, Your Highness."

He shrugged. "And you have a habit of assuming things that aren't true."

She felt her fingers curl around the arms of her chair as she tried to find her balance in a world that had suddenly been turned upside down just by his presence. And while he was here, she was suddenly conscious of the distance between them, a distance she knew she was responsible for and still wished she could breach.

"I'll, um, give you some privacy," Crystal said. Then, with

a quick smile for Marcus and a narrow-eyed look for her sister, she slipped out of the room.

"Why are you here, Marcus?"

He saw the wary hope in her eyes and wondered why he'd ever doubted his decision to come—and why he'd waited so long to do so. But she'd trampled all over his heart once already, and he wasn't going to make it so easy for her a second time. "Other than the auction, you mean?"

She shrugged. "If there is another reason."

"I came to see if you've grown up in the past couple of weeks," he said mildly.

Her eyes flashed. "I think you're forgetting which one of us is older than the other."

"And I think you're mistaking age with maturity."

"Is there a purpose to this conversation?"

"I just want you to know that I'm not going anywhere and I'm not giving up on us. We can make this work." He pinned her with his gaze. "If you're not afraid to go after what you really want."

He wouldn't have thought she'd balk at a challenge, but her eyes shifted away. Obviously he'd underestimated her obstinacy.

"I have everything I want right here," she told him.

"Do you?"

"Yes."

It was the defiant tilt of her chin that gave her away, and he couldn't help but smile. "It's always all or nothing with you, isn't it?"

"What's that supposed to mean?"

"You don't know how to compromise."

"I do so."

His brows rose; she frowned.

"You believe that giving a little means giving in. So rather than trying to work things out, you ran away."

"I tried," she said. "I just can't live my life the way you do."

"You shut me out."

"You let me!"

And the hurt and frustration in her voice took the edge off of his own anger. "And that's what it comes down to, doesn't it?"

She swallowed and looked away.

"Your father was a sonofabitch, Jewel. There's no denying that. He made you jump through hoops like no child should ever have to do, and still he withheld his love and affection."

"That's old news," she said.

"And then there was Thomas."

Her gaze swung back to his. "What do you know about Thomas?"

"I know he was the guy you ran off to the rodeo with, the one you thought you would marry, the one who wasn't willing to give up his nomadic lifestyle to settle down."

"Which proves that he never really loved me."

"Maybe he didn't," he said softly. "Or maybe he just wasn't willing to play your games.

"Maybe I did let you shut me out," he continued. "Maybe I was a little ticked off at being dumped and needed some time to figure things out, to decide if I was going to let you pull my strings."

"I wasn't—"

"Turns out I was," he interrupted. "At least this one time. Because I do love you, and because I realized you have a lot of insecurities about relationships and trust, so I'm willing to cut you some slack."

She stared at him. "Am I supposed to thank you for that?"

He ignored her sarcasm. "But from this point on—no more games, Jewel. No more excuses. I want a future with you, a life together. A baby." He saw her eyes grow wide, read the heartfelt yearning he knew she wished she could hide, and he smiled a little. "Maybe even two or three."

Her eyes filled with tears, though she valiantly held them in check.

"I've spent the past several years trying to figure out what I wanted," he told her. "I didn't have a clue until I met you. Now I'm just waiting for you to catch up."

"My brother Rowan proposed to his wife three times before she said 'yes.' I've decided that when I finally ask a woman to marry me, I'm only going to do it once. So I'm giving you some time, Jewel, to figure out if you want the same things I do, to decide if you're willing to compromise so that we can build our life together."

Marcus touched her face. "It won't be easy," he admitted. "I have duties and responsibilities to my country, but I respect that you have obligations here, and I know we can find a way to balance everything—if that's what you want."

It was the longest speech of his life—aside from any that had been prepared by one of the palace's press secretaries—and the most heartfelt. But when it was over, he knew he'd said everything he wanted to say. The rest was up to Jewel.

Jewel didn't see Marcus at all in the nine days leading up to the auction, though she knew he'd been busy promoting the event and giving interviews about Haven, no doubt trying to show her that the media attention she'd shunned could be used to advantage at times. And she could hardly object when the auction turned out to be a huge success.

She kept a mental tally of the bidding from the background, and she was more than a little stunned at the revenue that was being generated, and thrilled that Haven would be able to operate for at least another year. As for her own future, well, she wasn't so certain.

She'd thought long and hard about the things Marcus had said the last time they were together, and she'd realized he was right. She wouldn't go so far as to say that she'd been pulling his strings, as he claimed, but maybe she had been testing him, needing to know that she really mattered to him.

But for all of his talk of marriage and babies—and yeah, he had to know mentioning babies would make everything inside her turn to mush—he'd been nowhere to be found in the past week-and-a-half. And after agonizing over this fact for a while, she realized he was testing her, testing her trust in him and his love for her. And she finally accepted that he did love her—maybe even as much as she loved him. But was love enough to overcome the obstacles they would face? Because she knew that building a life with Marcus wouldn't be easy. Any marriage required adjustments and compromise; a union between a prince and a commoner would necessitate changes she probably couldn't even begin to imagine. There were so many things she didn't know, so many things they hadn't ever talked about.

She knew so little about his life as a royal, his responsibilities as a prince, his hopes and dreams.

I want a future with you, a life together. A baby.

On the other hand, maybe she knew everything she needed to.

She didn't delude herself into thinking it would be easy. She didn't want easy—she wanted Marcus.

There were a lot of details to figure out, but she wasn't going to figure them out backstage at an auction, and she certainly wasn't going to figure them out on her own. Whatever answers needed to be found, she and Marcus would find them together.

Now, she just needed to find him so she could tell him.

It was only when Crystal elbowed her in the ribs that the applause registered and Jewel realized the bidding on the last item had concluded. She smoothed a hand over her skirt and stepped onto the stage, figuring that she'd waited ten days to tell Marcus the truth of what was in her heart, she could surely wait another ten minutes.

She stepped up to the podium and spoke into the microphone. "I want to thank everyone for their generous and continued support of the Fourth Annual Haven Charity Auction. Tonight's event was an unprecedented success and your private contributions and successful bids will go a long way toward allowing Haven to continue its work as a rescue and rehabilitation facility. I'd also like to thank—"

"Please excuse the interruption," Natasha said, speaking into a microphone from the other side of the stage. "It appears we may have been a little premature in concluding this event."

Jewel was careful not to let her irritation show, though she wondered what kind of stunt the other woman had planned.

"There is one final item up for sale tonight that was added to our inventory at the last minute."

Nerves began to gnaw at the pit of Jewel's stomach, but she stayed where she was, her smile firmly in place.

A pedestal was carried out to center stage and set beneath the spotlight. An enlarged image was projected onto the wide screen against the back wall, and prompted several audible gasps and numerous "oohs" and "aahs."

The crowd pressed closer to the stage, as curious potential buyers sought a closer look at the stunning ring on display.

"I would like to call His Royal Highness Prince Marcus Santiago up here to tell us a little about this ring and the conditions attached to its sale here today."

Marcus stepped out from the wings, answering Jewel's question about where he had been, and making so many others swirl in her mind.

He took the spare microphone Natasha offered. "First I want to say that not only am I offering this ring today, but with it a check to Haven in the amount of one million dollars."

"A royal heirloom and a cool one mil for the charity," Natasha said. "Tell me, Your Highness, what is the catch?"

"I don't know that I would call it a catch so much as conditions that I've attached to the sale of this ring," he explained.

"You've got everyone's attention now," Natasha assured him, clearly in her element and playing to the crowd.

Marcus looked out at the assembled group and smiled. Then his gaze shifted across the stage to where Jewel was standing, and it was as if everyone else in the room faded away.

"It was my grandmother's ring," he said. "And when it was passed on to me, it was with the express wish that it remain in the family. So that is the first condition—the woman who buys this ring must marry me."

"I'll start the bidding," a female voice called out from the back of the crowd.

There were a few chuckles mixed in with various comments shouted back at the speaker.

"The second condition," Marcus said, interrupting the good-natured banter, "is that I will only sell the ring—and my proposal—to one particular woman."

There were good-natured groans and protests from the crowd, but no one walked away as the prince turned toward Jewel. No one wanted to miss the ending of this unexpected event.

Crystal stepped closer to nudge her sister forward, but Jewel felt as if her feet were glued to the floor.

"That woman," Marcus continued, "is Jewel Callahan."

She still couldn't move, so he started toward her. As he drew nearer, she could see, very clearly, the love shining in his eyes. And it was that which gave her courage, and helped her to meet him halfway.

Still, her stomach was a jumble of nerves and her voice wasn't quite steady when she said, "Did it never occur to you to propose like an ordinary person? Maybe over dinner by candlelight?"

He grinned. "I'm not ordinary—I'm a prince."

"I'm not likely to forget that," she assured him.

"So what do you think—" he took her hand and drew her over to the pedestal, to take a closer look at the ring "—do you want to bid on it?"

She had to clear her throat before she could speak. "How much?"

"The minimum bid is one dollar," he told her.

"I give you one dollar and you give me a check for a million?" She wondered if this was really a proposal or some kind of publicity stunt.

He shook his head. "I wouldn't want anyone to think I had to buy myself a bride. The check has already been made out to Haven. So the only question now is—do you want the ring?"

She didn't even look at the ring. She didn't care if it was a huge diamond in a platinum setting or a carved piece of tin, all that mattered was that she was going to spend the rest of her life with the man she loved.

"I want you," she told him softly.

He smiled. "Then you need to ante up."

She reached into her jacket for a dollar and flushed when she found her pockets were empty, save for the lucky stone she'd taken to carrying with her since the day Marcus had given it to her at the racetrack. She closed her fingers around it now. "I don't have any money."

Crystal pressed something into her other hand. "It's a five," she whispered. "It's all I've got."

Jewel took a deep breath and stared straight into Marcus's eyes—his beautiful, espresso-colored eyes that she wanted only to stare into every day for the rest of their lives together.

"I bid five dollars," she said. "And my whole heart, forever."

His hand closed over hers holding the money and he pulled her toward him and into his arms. Then he kissed her, as if he'd been waiting for weeks to do so. And she kissed him back, because she'd been waiting just as long.

And as the kiss deepened, they both forgot they were standing on the middle of the raised stage in front of a crowd of curious onlookers and eager media personnel.

"And that," Natasha announced, "concludes the Fourth Annual Haven Charity Auction."

As the crowd slowly filtered out, Jewel drew away.

"I never actually heard a proposal," she said to Marcus.

"Because I promised myself that I would only ask once, and I wanted to be sure of the answer before I did so."

"Are you sure now?"

He gazed into her eyes for a long moment before he finally nodded. Then he took the ring from the box and held it out to her. "Will you marry me, Jewel?"

And finally she had the chance to tell him everything that

was in her heart, but when she looked into his eyes, she realized that he already knew, that there was only one word he was waiting to hear from her.

"Yes."

He smiled as he slipped the ring on her finger, though she noted that his hand wasn't much steadier than hers, and Jewel's heart felt as if it would simply overflow with love and joy.

Then he kissed her again, and she knew that he felt exactly the same way.

When he finally drew away, she had to ask, "Did you really mean what you said about wanting babies?"

"I meant everything I said," he promised her.

"You do understand, with me being so much older than you, I'll want to get started on those babies as soon as possible."

He smiled again. "As soon as I get you home."

Epilogue

Prince's Bride Trades Stetson for Tiara
by Alex Girard

Last summer, Prince Marcus Santiago put his heart on public display along with an heirloom fourteen-carat diamond ring when he proposed to Jewel Callahan, former champion barrel racer turned owner of Callahan Thoroughbred Center in Alliston, West Virginia.

Yesterday, the prince regent's youngest brother and his cowgirl bride exchanged their vows.

As if a royal wedding wasn't enough cause for celebration, Prince Eric stood beside his brother at the altar, a remarkable feat considering it was less than a year ago that doctors weren't sure he would ever stand up again.

But all eyes were fixed on the bride as she made her

way up the center aisle of the cathedral in her stunning Vera Wang gown, a bundle of ivory tulips in hand. And none were focused so intently as those of her groom.

When the newlyweds rode off into the sunset together, there was no doubt that the beautiful horse-trainer had firmly lassoed her husband's heart—or that the prince had finally found his own crown Jewel.

* * * * *

Look for Prince Eric's story, the next chapter
in Brenda Harlen's miniseries
REIGNING MEN
After a brief but passionate affair,
Prince Eric Santiago is shocked to learn that the woman
he slept with is pregnant—with his child!
One thing's for sure—this Christmas will be
a holiday he'll never forget....
Don't miss
THE PRINCE'S HOLIDAY BABY
On sale December 2008,
wherever Silhouette Books are sold.

He cautioned himself to be leery. He was human and he'd been conned before. But never by anyone nearly so attractive. Never by anyone he'd felt so attracted to.

In her defense, Nick supposed that Georgie could actually be telling him the truth. That she was a victim in all this. He had his people back in California checking her out, to make sure she was who she said she was and had, as she claimed, not even been near a computer but on the road these last few months that the threats had been made.

In the meantime, he was doing his own checking out. Up close and exceedingly personal. So personal he could feel his blood stirring.

It had been a long time since he'd thought of himself as anything other than a law enforcement agent of one type or other. But Georgeann Grady made him remember that beneath the oaths he had taken and his devotion to duty, there beat the heart of a man.

A man who'd been far too long without the touch of a woman.

He watched as the light from the fireplace caressed the outline of Georgie's small, trim, jean-clad body as she moved about the rustic living room that could have easily come off the set of a Hollywood Western. Except that it was genuine.

As genuine as she claimed to be?

Something inside of him hoped so.

He wasn't supposed to be taking sides. His only interest in being here was to guarantee Senator Joe Colton's safety as the latter continued to make his bid for the presidency. Everything else was supposed to be secondary, but, Nick had to silently admit, that was just a wee bit hard to remember right now.

Earlier, before she'd put her precocious handful of a daughter to bed, Georgie had fed his appetite by whipping up some kind of a delicious concoction out of the vegetables she'd pulled from her garden. Vegetables that, by all rights should have been withered and dried. She'd mentioned that a friend came by on occasion to weed and tend it. Still, it surprised him that somehow she'd managed to make something mouthwatering out of it.

Almost as mouthwatering as she looked to him right at this moment.

Again, he was reminded of the appetite that hadn't been fed, hadn't been satisfied.

And wasn't going to be, Nick sternly told himself. At least not now. Maybe later, when things took on a more definite shape and all the questions in his head were answered to his satisfaction, there would be time to explore this feeling. This woman. But not now.

Damn it.

"Sorry about the lack of light," Georgie said, breaking into his train of thought as she turned around to face him. If she noticed the way he was looking at her, she gave no indication. "But I don't see a point in paying for electricity if I'm not going to be here. Besides, Emmie really enjoys camping out. She likes roughing it."

"And you?" Nick asked, moving closer to her, so close that a whisper would have trouble fitting in. "What do you like?"

The very breath stopped in Georgie's throat as she looked up at him.

"I think you've got a fair shot of guessing that one," she told him softly.

* * * * *

*Be sure to look for COLTON'S SECRET SERVICE
and the other following titles from*
THE COLTONS: FAMILY FIRST *miniseries:*
RANCHER'S REDEMPTION by Beth Cornelison
THE SHERIFF'S AMNESIAC BRIDE by Linda Conrad
SOLDIER'S SECRET CHILD by Caridad Piñeiro
BABY'S WATCH by Justine Davis
A HERO OF HER OWN by Carla Cassidy

Romantic
SUSPENSE

**Sparked by Danger,
Fueled by Passion.**

The Coltons Are Back!

Marie Ferrarella
Colton's Secret Service

The Coltons: Family First

On a mission to protect a senator, Secret Service agent
Nick Sheffield tracks down a threatening message only
to discover Georgie Gradie Colton, a rodeo-riding single
mom, who insists on her innocence. Nick is instantly
taken with the feisty redhead, but vows not to let his
feelings interfere with his mission. Now he must figure
out if this woman is conning him or if he can trust her
and the passion they share....

Available September wherever books are sold.

**Look for upcoming Colton titles
from Silhouette Romantic Suspense:**

RANCHER'S REDEMPTION by Beth Cornelison, Available October
THE SHERIFF'S AMNESIAC BRIDE by Linda Conrad, Available November
SOLDIER'S SECRET CHILD by Caridad Piñeiro, Available December
BABY'S WATCH by Justine Davis, Available January 2009
A HERO OF HER OWN by Carla Cassidy, Available February 2009

Visit Silhouette Books at www.eHarlequin.com SRS27598

Silhouette

SPECIAL EDITION

HEART OF STONE
by

DIANA PALMER

On sale September.

SAVE $1.⁰⁰ OFF

the Silhouette Special Edition® novel
HEART OF STONE on sale
September 2008, when you purchase
2 Silhouette Special Edition® books.

*Available wherever books are sold, including most
bookstores, supermarkets, drugstores and discount stores.*

Coupon expires December 31, 2008. Redeemable at participating
retail outlets in the U.S. only. Limit one coupon per customer.

5 65373 00076 2 (8100)0 11556

SSECPNUS0808

REQUEST YOUR FREE BOOKS!
2 FREE NOVELS PLUS 2 FREE GIFTS!

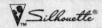

SPECIAL EDITION®
Life, Love and Family!

YES! Please send me 2 FREE Silhouette Special Edition® novels and my 2 FREE gifts (gifts are worth about $10). After receiving them, if I don't wish to receive any more books, I can return the shipping statement marked "cancel." If I don't cancel, I will receive 6 brand-new novels every month and be billed just $4.24 per book in the U.S. or $4.99 per book in Canada, plus 25¢ shipping and handling per book and applicable taxes, if any*. That's a savings of at least 15% off the cover price! I understand that accepting the 2 free books and gifts places me under no obligation to buy anything. I can always return a shipment and cancel at any time. Even if I never buy another book from Silhouette, the two free books and gifts are mine to keep forever.

235 SDN EEYU   335 SDN EEY6

Name	(PLEASE PRINT)	
Address		Apt. #
City	State/Prov.	Zip/Postal Code

Signature (if under 18, a parent or guardian must sign)

Mail to the Silhouette Reader Service:
IN U.S.A.: P.O. Box 1867, Buffalo, NY 14240-1867
IN CANADA: P.O. Box 609, Fort Erie, Ontario L2A 5X3

Not valid to current subscribers of Silhouette Special Edition books.

Want to try two free books from another line?
Call 1-800-873-8635 or visit www.morefreebooks.com.

* Terms and prices subject to change without notice. N.Y. residents add applicable sales tax. Canadian residents will be charged applicable provincial taxes and GST. Offer not valid in Quebec. This offer is limited to one order per household. All orders subject to approval. Credit or debit balances in a customer's account(s) may be offset by any other outstanding balance owed by or to the customer. Please allow 4 to 6 weeks for delivery. Offer available while quantities last.

Your Privacy: Silhouette is committed to protecting your privacy. Our Privacy Policy is available online at www.eHarlequin.com or upon request from the Reader Service. From time to time we make our lists of customers available to reputable third parties who may have a product or service of interest to you. If you would prefer we not share your name and address, please check here. ☐

SSE08R

Silhouette®

SPECIAL EDITION

HEART OF STONE

by

DIANA PALMER

On sale September.

SAVE $1.00 OFF

the Silhouette Special Edition® novel
HEART OF STONE on sale
September 2008, when you purchase
2 Silhouette Special Edition® books.

Available wherever books are sold, including most bookstores, supermarkets, drugstores and discount stores.

Coupon expires December 31, 2008. Redeemable at participating retail outlets in Canada only. Limit one coupon per customer.

CANADIAN RETAILERS: Harlequin Enterprises Limited will pay the face value of this coupon plus 10.25¢ if submitted by the customer for this specified product only. Any other use constitutes fraud. Coupon is nonassignable. Void if taxed, prohibited or restricted by law. Void if copied. Consumer must pay any government taxes. Nielsen Clearing House customers ("NCH") submit coupons and proof of sales to Harlequin Enterprises Limited, P.O. Box 3000, Saint John, NB E2L 4L3, Canada. Non–NCH retailer: for reimbursement, submit coupons and proof of sales directly to Harlequin Enterprises Limited, Retail Marketing Department, 225 Duncan Mill Rd., Don Mills (Toronto), ON M3B 3K9, Canada. Limit one coupon per purchase. Valid in Canada only.

52608458

SSECPNCDN0808

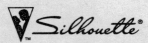

COMING NEXT MONTH

#1921 HEART OF STONE—Diana Palmer
Businessman rancher Boone Sinclair had it all—except for Keely Walsh. But from the first time he saw her on his property, he was determined not to let her get away…because every Long, Tall Texan gets his way, and this one would not be denied!

#1922 THE RANCHER'S SURPRISE MARRIAGE
Susan Crosby
Back in Business
When her fiancé dumped her on the eve of their high-profile wedding, movie star Maggie McShane needed to save major face. Luckily, local rancher Tony Young agreed to a staged ceremony that would rescue her image. But then their feelings became more than mere Hollywood fantasy, and Tony rescued the starlet's heart as well.…

#1923 HITCHED TO THE HORSEMAN—Stella Bagwell
Men of the West
After a stint in the air force and a string of bad-news breakups, ranching heiress Mercedes Saddler headed back to her hometown a little world-weary. That's when Gabe Trevino, the new horse trainer on her family's ranch, gave her the boost she needed…and a real shot at true love.

#1924 EXPECTING THE DOCTOR'S BABY
Teresa Southwick
Men of Mercy Medical
Management coach Samantha Ryan wanted unconditional love; E.R. doc Mitch Tenney wanted no strings attached. A night of passion gave them both more than they bargained for. Now what would they do?

#1925 THE DADDY VERDICT—Karen Rose Smith
Dads in Progress
The day Sierra Girard broke the news that she was having district attorney Ben Barclay's baby, he didn't know which end was up. Commitment and trust just weren't his thing. But then a case he was working on threatened Sierra's safety, and Ben realized he'd reached a verdict—guilty of loving the mommy-to-be in the first degree!

#1926 THE BRIDESMAID'S TURN—Nicole Foster
The Brothers of Rancho Pintada
Just when architect Aria Charez had given up looking for Mr. Right, Cruz Declan came to town. Visiting Rancho Pintada to meet his long-lost father and brothers, the successful engineer was soon overwhelmed by newfound family…until newfound love-of-his-life Aria made it all worthwhile.

SSECNM0808